THE DARK EDEN

THE DARK EDEN

ASIN:B08JF17PZ2

Cover my Damoro Designs

Publisher: Wicked Storm Publishing, LLC

Chapter One

They say that hindsight is 20/20. That you can look back on something and see it clearer than you did in the moment. But what happens when you look back on your vengeance and you don't regret a single thing?

Hindsight is 20/20, after all.

I remember what happened, every last second of it. The hurt, the betrayal, the fire and the darkness that it all plunged me into.

My darkness.

The thing that I had spent my entire life running from had finally caught up to me. No amount of running could save me from the monsters that lurked in the shadows, because the monsters were I.

I didn't know how long I'd been out for, or if I'd even ever wake up, so there I lay, swimming in the scalding embrace of my own mind.

My chest ached and my lungs burned like someone had set them ablaze. My skin sizzled from the fire magic that seemed to be burning me from the inside out.

I didn't fight it, how could I?

Part of me felt like I deserved it— like it was the penance to be paid for my ferocious sins. My mind traveled back to the moment when it happened, when I finally snapped and the fire magic inside of me erupted in all directions.

But even so, the part of me that felt like I deserved it was nothing but a sliver compared to the part of me that still raged with anger. That was the part that scared me the most, the one that felt no remorse for what I'd done.

The part that would do it again in a heartbeat.

***

I was jolted awake by a wave of excruciating pain. I sat straight up gasping for air and clawing at my throat as the air made its way into my lungs. I coughed and gagged, every breath feeling like a new bucket of hot coals being shoved into my throat.

My skin burned, and the space behind my eyes felt like it was being prodded with a scalding poker.

I stumbled off of the bed and scrambled to my feet just in time to see the comforter go up in flames. The fire spread and began eating away the bed.

Everything inside my head was a blur, covered by the haze of sleep that still hung heavily over me. If it were just me there, the entire room would have been up in flames in a few mere minutes, but I was relieved when a thick stream of water shot from the corner of the room and doused the bed, and the flames, to nothing but a smoldering smoke.

I had never been more thankful to see Apollo's smug face since the moment I'd met him.

Just when I thought that the nightmare was over, I reached out for Apollo, mortified to see both of my arms blazing with flames. The flames danced across my skin, leaving a searing pain in their wake.

I screamed in agony, almost too overwhelmed with pain to notice Apollo pulling another thick stream of water from a bucket that lay beside him. The look on his face was grim as his eyes shifted to mine.

I could have sworn for a split second I saw a glimmer of empathy embedded in his icy blue pools, but I had to have been mistaken. That wasn't Apollo's style.

Hot tears streamed down my face, leaving yet another trail of searing pain behind them, and spiraled to the floor. I looked down to see the droplets of fire spiraling before colliding with the hardwood and commencing their task of eating away at it too.

Fire.

I was crying fire.

I was on fire.

I *was* fire.

The pain was so deep that the realizations were short. I couldn't think, I couldn't breathe, and I caught myself wishing that I could just return to the darkness.

"Apollo, help me." I managed to get the words out as more tears of flame leaked from my eyes.

The look on Apollo's face was a broken one. For once I didn't see a single drop of sarcasm or smugness grace his features. All I saw through the blaze of blurry tears was how tightly he clenched his jaw. I couldn't figure out what about him was so different. Why he had gone from looking at me like I was a nuisance, to looking at me like a delicate butterfly that he was trying to capture in a net.

But I didn't have enough energy to keep fighting the pain and find the strength to care at the same time.

"I'm sorry, Eden." Apollo said the words so softly that I almost couldn't make out what they were.

I didn't understand why he was sorry until I saw the stream of water heading for me. The water morphed into an orb as big as my crumpled body, and before I knew what was happening it engulfed me completely.

There was a cooling sensation that hit every inch of my skin so fast that it hurt. I opened my mouth to scream out in pain, but all I got was a mouthful of water.

My skin completely simmered until the burning subsided completely, which was when the orb of water released me from its hold.

My body collapsed to the ground. I coughed and gagged until the water that had invaded my lungs had crawled its way back up my throat and I could breathe somewhat regularly again.

I lay on the ground, soaked. It took me a few seconds of deep breaths before I realized that I was completely naked, just when Adler and Atlas burst through the door.

"Oh my gods, Eden! Are you okay?" Atlas scrambled to help me up, but I rushed backward until my back pressed up against the bed.

Atlas put both hands in the air and backed away from me slowly, his grey eyes full of pain. "Hey, hey, hey. You're okay. You're okay." He assured me.

I ripped what was left of the comforter off the bed and down onto my body to preserve whatever decency I had left.

My eyes darted around the room nervously from each guy to another. There was just too much going on for my mind to fully process, so there I sat, soaked and freezing. But after the hell I'd just endured, I gladly accepted the cold over any type of heat.

As hard as I tried, I couldn't form a word, but even if I had been able to I was sure that it would have been barely intelligible because of how violently I shivered.

"What the hell happened to her?" Adler asked.

Atlas and Adler both turned to Apollo, looking for an answer. Apollo still looked broken, traumatized by what he'd seen. His normally tan face now was pale and there was a distant look in his eyes. By the look of him, you would have thought that he was the

8

one who was almost burned to a crisp, not me.

"I don't know." Apollo finally got the words out as he managed to lower himself back into the armchair that sat in the corner. "One minute she was sleeping like she has been for the past week, and the next minute the bed was on fire, and so was she."

A week? The words hit me like a ton of bricks. There was no way I could have been trapped in the darkness for a week, was there?

That's the kind of thing that you think you'd be able to tell, but the truth was that I had no idea how long I was trapped inside my head, tortured by my thoughts.

"We left you with her for one night and this is what happens, dude?" It was the first time that I'd ever heard laid-back Adler sound anywhere near angry or upset.

Up until then I didn't know if he was even capable of feeling those things.

Apollo's eyes snapped back up from the place they had been focused on the floor and the fire was ablaze in them once again. There he was, the old Apollo who didn't take crap from anyone.

"You're lucky I *was* the one who was here. What would you have done? Thrown plants on her? Or Atlas? Blew wind on her and added more oxygen to the flames?" His voice was raised and his chest was puffed.

And just like that every ounce of vulnerability he had almost shown flew out the window.

Adler said something in return, but at that point I had drowned their useless squabbling out. I pulled my arms out from beneath the blanket and held them shakily in front of me inspecting my skin. With the amount of pain that I'd felt, I would have bet my life on the fact that it should have left behind burn marks. It should have left a scar, or a welt, or even just a red mark.

But my skin was just as smooth and normal as it had always been.

"Why did it hurt?" The words fell shakily from my lips, and they were only a whisper but the fact that I'd said anything at all halted the argument.

Atlas slowly approached me, careful not to overstep any invisible boundaries. He crouched down and waited patiently for my eyes to rise up to meet his gaze. He held a smile, and his dimples indented into his smooth brown skin. There was a soft feeling of understanding in his eyes, a feeling that made me feel like I could take all the time that I needed to muster the energy to find my voice again. I knew he'd wait.

"I said, why did it hurt?" I repeated my question, my voice a lot less shaky the second time around.

I still held my arms out in front of me twisting them to get a look at every inch of my forearms, still searching for a blemish that wasn't there.

"I told you, fire magic is different from all the rest." Apollo said from across the room.

"What Apollo is trying to say," Atlas corrected him with a soft tone. "Is that fire magic is the most potent elemental magic there is. Its power comes at a price for those who wield it. That price is your pain and sanity."

His words shook me to my core.

My pain and sanity. Two things that I didn't sign up to hand out like candy to the mystical forces.

Better yet, I didn't sign up for this at all. I never asked to be the eden, the magical catch all— all I wanted was a lick of magic to balance me with everyone else.

But when I begged the universe for that, I meant the ability to bend the stream of water coming out of a faucet or to magically brew coffee at the shop.

Not to have all four freaking elements at once!

The entire thing was insane.

I thought back to Asher, and how he commanded fire as easily as he breathed. He held it in his hands and danced in the flames without flinching a single time.

"How is Asher able to do it without pain?" I asked the question out loud, but it was more of a question to the universe, or the gods, or whoever the heck was in charge of the magical system.

I really wanted to know, how had he found a cheat?

"He isn't." Apollo answered so quickly that I knew he didn't even have to think. "I told you when his magic came in, he changed. There was a reason for it."

Apollo clenched his jaw tightly once again, revealing the small vein that ran up the side of his neck and stopped just underneath his chiseled jawline when he was upset.

Suddenly I understood why Asher was such a psycho. Why he

wanted to cause pain to everybody.

The pain I'd felt was excruciating, and it was only for a few moments. I couldn't imagine living with it for years.

What that must have done to his head was the scariest part of all.

Thinking of Asher brought me to thinking of Jade, and I felt my fists clench before I even realized what I was doing.

Jade, my best friend, the person whom I trusted more than anything in the world, had shattered my heart into a million pieces. It was her who had hurt me deep enough to explode whatever container was holding back the fire magic inside of me. It was her who released its agony in my body.

It was all her.

Every inch of my body ached because of her.

A wave of anger roared up in the pit of my stomach, and it was scalding hot. I wanted nothing more than to find her and punch her in the face with my flaming fist. Maybe then she would understand the pain that she caused me.

The anger ate away at my inside so ferociously that I caught myself gritting my teeth, and before I knew it my fist burst into flames and I screamed out into pain.

In an instant, Apollo used his water whip to douse my fist, sending an even greater wave of pain through my hand.

"Eden," Adler interjected quickly. "You need to get a grip on your emotions before you burn the entire manor down."

I didn't want to admit it, but Adler was right. If I didn't get myself in check quickly, I wouldn't be the only person who felt the agony of burning flesh.

I was mad at the world, but I wasn't mad at the guys. They didn't deserve to share my fate.

I jumped to my feet, still clinging to the tattered blanket.

"I should go home. You guys aren't safe when I'm with you."

A mortified look came over each of their faces, I almost didn't dare to ask.

"Eden, you don't remember?" Atlas laid a hand on my arm, and I noticed his hand was freezing cold compared to the temperature of my skin.

It was a nice contrast, but I couldn't enjoy it fully because my mind immediately went into overdrive trying to figure out what he was talking about.

I remembered the fight, and I remembered my fire magic coming into play. But what did I care if my house was a little torched? Even better, because no one would notice if I accidentally burned a few things here and there.

I raised a brow, quietly analyzing the looks on their faces.

"Eden, you can't go home. It's burned." Adler reminded me gently.

"I know, I don't care. This blanket's burned, but it still works." I shrugged.

"Eden, I don't think you understand." Atlas added too, still gently tiptoeing around my feelings.

"You burned the entire city to the ground." Apollo huffed, ripping off the emotional Band-Aid all at once.

"What?" I murmured, stumbling backward. "That can't be true."

I backed up until my back pressed against the smooth wall.

Around me it felt like the walls were closing in, threatening to suffocate me. My chest heaved and my lungs felt like they were getting smothered.

A buzzing sensation danced across my skin, and all it did was make me even more nervous.

Was I only a few seconds away from burning down the manor too?

I ran past Adler and out into the hall. I didn't know where I was going, but I wasn't going to stop running until I did.

Chapter Two

I rushed through the hallways of the manor, careful not to touch a thing as I ran by.

My mind was a blur of anxious thoughts all feeding off the emotions that swirled around in my chest. As ferocious as they were, they still didn't light a candle to the anger that still festered inside of me.

Anger at the world for pushing my parents away from me, anger toward Jade for casting me aside like everyone else did, but more importantly anger toward Asher for pushing me as far as he could until I broke.

Asher wielded fire magic too. He knew better than anyone else the pain that it would cause, and he hunted me down and coaxed it out of me like a wild animal, waiting for a chance to see the light of day. The city being reduced to a mere pile of ash was just as much his fault as it was mine.

Maybe even more.

I shuffled down the halls, still clinging to what was left of the tattered blanket, praying that none of the water spectre servants or maids happened across me mid-meltdown. Out of all the people my fire magic was dangerous to, it was toward the creatures made of water.

Or was it the other way around?

I wasn't sure. Everything about magic was new to me, and that was on top of the fire- throwing psycho and the city that was burned to a crisp.

I had a lot on my plate.

I sneakily poked my head into the kitchen where the cooks prepared a meal. I watched curiously as they scurried around, the shine of the sun shimmering through their bodies made of water.

Probably scrambling for something to feed me, no doubt. I thought.

I knew news of my waking would spread like wildfire the second I ran from the room, no pun intended. The last thing I wanted was a plethora of people weighing me down with their questions, and I especially didn't want Jonathon to get his claws in me. I'd only known him for a small time, but I had a feeling that guilt-tripping was one of his hidden powers, and that was a power that I didn't have a defense to at the time.

A cook scurried past the doorway and I hurriedly pulled my head back into the hallway. My lungs stung from the breath I held so tightly, but I couldn't chance it. I didn't dare move a muscle until I knew the coast was clear, and when it was, I sprinted across the kitchen and managed to slip through the glass double doors, finding my freedom in the grassy backyard. I ran for a few seconds until there was enough space between the house and I before I dared to slow my stride. The sun shone down hot against the bare skin of my shoulders and face, but even the waves of heat were nothing compared to the intense heat that had nearly fried my skin. I actually welcomed the cool contrast.

When I finally stopped sprinting, I slowed to a stop to catch my breath before collapsing in the sea of warm green grass. Up ahead the Temple of Eden stood prominently, beckoning to me but I didn't have the energy to even consider answering the call. I was way weaker than I'd ever been, and that scared me. I let out a rough sigh and let my arms fall to my sides, the blades of grass tickling my skin. My gaze fell on the sky and its cool tone of baby blue.

I wish I could fly. My eyes trailed the fluffy white clouds as they slowly cut their way through the sky on the relaxed breeze. *Maybe it would solve everything.*

I closed my eyes and imagined being able to float with the breeze. I wished I could just pick up and float off to a distant land. One without magic, or elemental classes— one without edens.

"I never asked for this." I huffed out loud. "I never wanted any of this!"

"You may not have asked for it, but you got it."

I turned to see Atlas towering beside me with his hands shoved casually in his pockets.

"Holy crap, I didn't even hear you coming." My heart skipped a beat at the sight of him.

"One of the perks of being able to literally walk on air." Atlas shrugged before stopping to take a seat beside me.

I adjusted what was left of my tattered blanket, trying to shift my attention to anything but the way the look in his smoky grey eyes made me feel.

Ever since I had sex with Apollo, I noticed new things about the guys. At first it was subtle like the way Adler's laugh made my body tingle in places that I couldn't ignore, but the more time that went by, the more my body screamed for them every time they were near. It was like a spark lighting everywhere inside my body instead of just my eyes.

For Atlas it was *his* eyes. They were two pools of seduction that had the power to make me squirm with just a gaze.

It wasn't his fault. It wasn't like he was trying to get me to take my pants off, they just happened to want to drop to the floor every time our eyes met.

I guess I'm safe, because I'm technically not even wearing pants.

Out of the corner of my eye I noticed Atlas's undivided attention on me, and my cheeks started to simmer a shade of pink.

"You know," Atlas' smooth voice broke the stale silence that hung between us. "A lot of times I look at you and wonder what it is that's going through that beautiful head of yours."

His words only made my cheeks burn brighter, and I worried that my fire magic was going to pip in and add to the misery.

"What do you mean?" I asked with my eyes still skimming the wandering clouds above.

I didn't dare to look at him out of fear that if I did he might actually be able to guess what I was thinking. I didn't need him knowing that I wanted nothing more than to be naked with him, nothing holding our bare bodies back.

Atlas sighed and slid down to lie on his back beside me in the dewy grass. He slid his arms behind his head and scooted in close enough that his rib cage pressed against the side of my body, with only the tattered blanket keeping us apart.

He was so close that I could smell the scent of his cologne as it danced across his skin. I fought the urge to run my fingertips across his body.

Get a hold of yourself Eden! I tore my eyes from his torso and shifted my weight in an attempt to ignore the messages my body was screaming at me.

Atlas closed his eyes and his tanned skin soaked in the sunlight.

"You have so much power. More than Adler, Apollo and I combined." He said it without a single wave of doubt in his tone. "Power like that could change the world, tear down kingdoms and build new ones all in the same breath. But you seem like you don't even want it."

I held on to each word as it snaked its way from between his lips, holding on to them for dear life.

"Because I don't." I answered so quickly, too quickly for my brain to filter the answer.

It came from a real, raw place deep inside of me. One that I wasn't always comfortable to show.

I looked up to gauge Atlas' expression, worried that my truth would shock him or drive him away. But there he sat, still soaking in every ray the sun was willing to lend him. His expression was soft and unbothered by a single thing I said.

It was an odd emotion feeling like I had free rein to say how I felt. I was so used to people scrutinizing every move I made. I didn't know what it was like for someone to care enough about you to let you be yourself and have your own opinions judgment free.

The more I thought about it, the more even Jade dictated how I felt and what I did. The fear of upsetting or losing her was a prison all in itself.

But it was different with Atlas. I could tell he was more interested in getting to know who I was as opposed to trying to shape who I was, and that was something that I hadn't had the pleasure of experiencing.

I waited for a response or a rebuttal. Maybe even an argument about how I was lucky and should be grateful for the crap show that fate had turned my life into.

Instead he sat peacefully, giving me time to collect my thoughts and waiting for me to articulate them.

And because of that, I swooned again. Atlas was so warm, welcoming, and patient. All things that I knew I needed trying to work my way through my fire magic.

I sighed, trying to sort through my emotions.

"I just don't understand why it had to be me."

I paused, waiting for Atlas to say something, but he didn't utter a word.

"It's just– I'm not the smartest person in the world. I'm not the prettiest person in the world. I'm definitely not the most successful person in the world. It's hard for me to understand why all this power, and these crazy prophecies were destined for me. *Me.* The same Eden who sat alone in the cafeteria most days because she only had one friend who was never at school. The same Eden who was always the last person chosen for sports and group projects. I'm not the girl with friends, or family, or even freaking confidence. I'm just— *me."*

The words that flowed from my lips were cathartic. I was spewing emotions that had been pent up for years and I didn't even know it. Things that I swore to myself didn't bother me were coming to the surface, and it felt good to finally be honest with myself about being bothered by them. It was like once I opened my mouth and let a few out, they all fought to tumble out into existence.

"I'm nothing special. Even Jade threw me away without a single thought." This time my words tangled up my stomach in a knotted mess as they made their way up my throat, leaving a sick and heavy feeling behind.

Tears threatened to escape my eyes.

My fists clenched tightly, and the simmer returned underneath my skin, only seconds away from setting my body ablaze again.

"There it is." Atlas said, finally breaking his vow of silence.

"There is what?"

"One of your triggers." Atlas scooted his body to the side to put a little distance between us, a protective measure from the heat that had started to radiate from my body once again.

I finally looked at him with confusion, and his gaze met mine. With one look I felt my attention shift from the past to the present. I was pulled from my anger, and my hatred, and all I could think about was his warm grey eyes, and me being the only thing to hold his attention.

"When you first get your magic it's hard to control. Most people are young when it shows up, so it's already hard enough to separate from your emotions. It's a reflex that we have, just like pulling a hand away from a hot stove, or reaching out to catch something that's falling without thinking. And we develop emotional triggers at times, thoughts or actions that our body reacts to with magic, without thinking."

I tried so hard to focus on the words that were coming from his mouth, but I got too fixated on his mouth itself. His lips looked so soft and plump. I couldn't keep myself from wondering how they'd feel pressed against mine.

"Once you're aware of the things that trigger that response though, you can start to combat it."

"Mhmhm." I mumbled, halfway acknowledging that I'd heard what he'd said. "Jade is a no-no."

Atlas smiled and his white teeth shone brightly.

"Are you even listening to what I'm saying anymore?" His smile shifted to a half smirk and his eyes flitted from my eyes, to my lips and back to my eyes.

Watching his gaze jump across my body sent me spiraling to an edge that I didn't know I was heading for— a point of no return.

The old Eden would have ignored her urges, probably even pretended they weren't there.

But the beast inside of me had been awoken.

"I'm listening to more than the words that you're saying." My voice was nearly a whisper now.

I slowly leaned in, and Atlas did the same until our lips met, sending an explosion of pleasure through my body.

I definitely wasn't going to ignore my urges ever again.

Chapter Three

Atlas' lips were as soft as my wildest imagination had led me to believe. The moment our lips touched there was a magical electricity that sparked between them, and the very second it happened I had no doubt that he was my spark.

I didn't know how it was possible for someone to spark with more than one person, but I didn't care. All I cared about were his lips pressed against mine, and what it did to me.

The kiss started out as a peck. It was just supposed to be a small test of the spark that I'd felt, a way to finally get my body to leave me alone constantly screaming sexual desires at me while I was in his presence. But it quickly snowballed from a peck into a drawn-out show of passion. I rolled to my side to meet him halfway, and our lips glided across each other in a tangle of spark and heat.

Inside a tornado of magic and emotion swirled together, threatening to morph into a full-blown hurricane if I didn't mind its power.

I brought my fingertips to rest on the bare skin of his arm, left exposed by the sleeves of his plain white T-shirt. His skin was as soft and warm as I'd imagined it too.

I felt him stir beneath the touch of my bare skin. It had nothing to do with the fact that I was nearly naked in front of him or that we were even kissing. It was the feeling I got when our skin touched, like fireworks being set off in my chest. I knew he had to feel it too. It was the same feeling I got whenever Apollo touched me, no matter how much he made me angry. There was no doubting the mystical connection that held us all together.

I parted my lips and my tongue made its way into Atlas' mouth, the tips tingled when they touched.

I felt his lips stretch into a smile mid kiss, and it was one of the most wholesome things I'd had the pleasure of experiencing.

He pulled away from our kiss and looked me in the eyes, his hand finding my face to brush away a misplaced strand of hair that had gotten stuck to my lip.

His touch nearly paralyzed me with pleasure. Who knew that the cheekbones were such a sexual hot spot. It was one of those things that you don't figure out until you're lying in the grass naked with your fated mate. One of the things that sounds weird until you experience it yourself, and I was experiencing it alright.

And I wanted to experience it over, and over, and over again until my cheeks were raw and numb.

"You are the most beautiful person whom I've ever had the pleasure of kissing, Eden." Atlas' eyes were glued to mine when he said the words, and his gaze didn't waver a single second.

I knew he was telling the truth, and somehow that made the touch of his skin feel even better.

I hadn't known him long, but he had already shown me more compassion and kindness than almost every person in my life. He even outshone Apollo, who would rather be buried with his sarcasm and emotional walls than let go of them for a single second.

Atlas was different. He was strong, but with soft edges. It was a combination that even I would have sworn could never work until I saw him pull it off with my own eyes.

"And you're one of only two people I've ever had the pleasure of kissing." I couldn't help but laugh as the words fell from my lips.

Atlas laughed too.

Other people would have cringed at what I'd said. It would have surely ruined the mood, but Atlas embraced it in a way that was more genuine than anything I'd ever seen.

That was when I knew that he was one of the people I could see myself spending the rest of my life with. One of the people whom I didn't have to fear giving my heart to because he'd rather die than watch me suffer a broken heart, and that was a feeling that I'd never had the pleasure of experiencing until that moment.

Atlas' hand found its way to the back of my head and he gently leaned me into his kiss, our lips meeting in the middle.

This time the kiss was sweet around the edges with a blaze of red-hot passion tangled between us. His fingertips ran up the length of my back that the tattered blanket had left exposed.

I squirmed underneath his touch and pulled away from the kiss to inhale sharply.

His smile returned at the sight of what his touch did to me.

I wanted to lean in and give him my all, but in the middle of the yard I felt more exposed than I did secure. The last thing I needed was the cooks getting a free show.

An idea popped into my head that had me jump to my feet. My eyes quickly darted to the temple and back to Atlas.

Before I had time to comprehend what was going on, Atlas' eyes turned completely white, and he commanded a gust of wind beneath him strong enough to lift him to his feet and push his body against mine. The second we were close enough, he pulled me in for another kiss that threatened to melt me where I stood and diminish me into a puddle.

"Show off." I muttered with a smile on my face the second I had time to come up for air.

"Me? Never." Atlas pulled my body in closely to his.

Beneath us, a swirl of air materialized like a tornado. Its gust was strong enough to lift both of our feet from the ground. I squeezed the sides of his arms so tightly that my knuckles showed white, and all he could do was chuckle at the look on my face.

"I guess this brings an entirely new meaning to being swept off your feet."

The gust dropped us right on the front doorstep of the temple, and I wobbled trying to steady my stance on the tile.

I pushed the heavy door open and we snuck inside, as quickly as we could before anyone from the house had time to notice. The door closed tightly, which engulfed us in a warm darkness.

I reached behind and fumbled awkwardly until my hand connected with something. I ran my fingers over the top and squeezed it, hoping to find Atlas' hand, but instead I was met with the stiff bulge that pressed against the fabric of his pants.

"Oh my gods, I'm sorry. I thought that was your hand. I–" I scrambled for an apology.

My eyes slowly started to adjust to the darkness and I could finally make out the shape of him standing in front of me.

He must have adapted to the lack of light a lot quicker than me because he reached out and was able to wrap his fingers around my wrist on the first try.

"Don't be sorry." His words were soft, but the bulge he pulled my hand back to was hard.

By then my eyes were nearly completely adjusted to the darkness, and I was able to see his warm grey eyes again, and they were looking directly into my soul.

If I could see him, I knew he could see me too, which meant that he could see the mortified look on my face.

I had only ever done anything sexual once, with Apollo. And

that was such a spur of the moment ordeal that I didn't have time to process it. I didn't have time to get nervous, and I sure as hell didn't have time to think about what I was doing.

I did now, and I was terrified.

Was I any good the last time? What did I even do? What did he do?

The questions bombarded my mind. I breathed quickly, and I felt like my chest was under attack by a boa constrictor. I didn't want to look stupid in front of Atlas, and I understood that there were some things that instinct ruled, but I had no idea where to start. My mind was a blank slate.

An embarrassing, inexperienced, nervous blank slate.

"I– I don't–"

"Shh." Atlas' finger pressed against my lips, halting the train wreck of words that was about to spill from my lips. He leaned in beside my ear, his lips so close I could feel his warm breath creeping down my neck. "I'll show you how. Is that okay?"

I swallowed hard and nodded, adding in a quick murmur just in case he didn't see.

"At any point we can stop, okay? You just have to tell me. As long as you're comfortable, I'm comfortable. Got it?"

He brought his hand to the side of my face and cupped it gently. The tone in his voice was so caring and thoughtful, two things that I didn't know could turn me on until I felt the tingle rest between my legs as my sweet spot started to salivate at the sound of his voice.

"Yes."

He gently tugged on the remains of the blanket that had barely held to my body, leaving me completely naked.

Even so, I didn't feel exposed like I thought I would. I didn't feel like seeing me in my most potent, and natural form was anything dirty. With Atlas it was different. It wasn't dirty, or sexual, or any other thing that might put even the slightest negative connotation on it.

No, with Atlas James it was spiritual. It was about allowing him to see me at my most vulnerable state, naked emotionally and physically, and letting him find all the ways he could think of to spread love across the blank canvas that was my body.

He spread the blanket out against the cold stones of the floor and motioned for me to lie on it. I could still feel a hint of the cold stone beneath the blanket against my bare back as I got comfortable, but at that point I wouldn't have cared if there was an entire boulder underneath my back. The anticipation of what was to come next was more than enough to distract me from anything.

Chapter Four

I got comfortable on my back and looked up just in time to get a good view of Atlas unbuckling his jeans and letting them drop to the floor, bringing his boxers with them.

His shirt had come off some time while I was getting comfortable on the ground, so there he stood, naked too. I let my eyes roam his body, starting at the defined muscles in his legs and working my way up to his dick that stood straight and stiff. It was definitely bigger than I'd ever imagined and way thicker too. I salivated just at the sight, but part of me wondered if I'd be able to handle it. It was only the second time I'd had sex in my entire life. What if I wasn't skilled enough to take that much? There was no mistaking he was bigger than Apollo.

I ripped my eyes from his manhood and let them linger on his toned stomach for a few seconds longer than necessary before my gaze drifted over his muscular chest too. Finally they made their way back up to his gorgeous face.

He smiled warmly like he always did, but there was something different inside his eyes. It was something primal that lingered there. I could tell that even with all his patience, he was having trouble keeping his urges in control. The sight of me lying naked on the ground was driving him mad.

He made his way to the floor and my legs parted like the Red Sea, ready to let him crawl between them.

"Are you sure you're ready for this?" He asked, lightly brushing my cheek with the tip of his finger.

"More sure than anything in my entire life." My words came out quickly, but I didn't even care if I sounded desperate— because I was.

The fire magic roared inside of me, stirring with the flames of my sexual urges. Together they were a hot mix, one that I was afraid would send my magic over the edge once again pushing me to burn things.

Atlas crawled between my open legs and positioned himself on top of me.

"You're even more beautiful naked than you are clothed." He said softly. "Which I didn't think was possible."

I took a second, trying to figure out if I should have been flattered or offended. I never got a chance to come to a conclusion, though, because his cool fingertips found their way to my hip bones and he trailed them up my side, tracing the subtle curve of my body. I let out a small sigh, a mix of relief and pleasure, as his hand ended up on my breast. My nipple immediately stiffened at the feel of his soft skin brushing against mine. He gently squeezed and a moan escaped my lips just before I pulled him in for another kiss.

There was a rush of energy sweeping through my body, one so potent that I felt like it was seeping out of my pores— lust.

In that moment I wanted nothing more than I wanted him to take me. I wanted him to take every inch of my being and use it for his pleasure— to split me open and weave himself inside of me.

I kissed him like I'd never kissed anyone before, my lips a tingling mess of magic and mischief. The longer my lips bumped against his, the more comfortable I felt. It was like all my hesitations melted to a pool on the ground, leaving nothing but my desires to take center stage.

I reached between us and fumbled in the dark awkwardly until my fingers brushed up against his dick, his skin stretched tightly by his erection. A small gasp fell from my mouth at the realization that it was even bigger than it had looked.

"Is everything okay?" Atlas pulled away from our kiss and looked into my eyes.

It was a beautiful sight to see him like that, perched over the top of me, with nothing holding out bodies back.

My cheeks grew warm. "I– I'm just not completely sure on what to do." I felt stupid saying the words, but it was true. With Apollo, it was so rushed and instinctual, and if I were being honest, I felt like he carried most of the load.

This time was different. I wanted to experience every inch of Atlas' body. I craved to feel him inside of me. I couldn't think of a single thing in the world that I wanted more.

Atlas smiled so brightly that it almost lit up the room. If it had been anyone else, I would have died of embarrassment at the admission, but I knew that Atlas would understand. There wasn't a better person in the universe to learn and explore with. I trusted him with my body and my emotions. Even when they were all over the place like they were then.

Atlas pulled me in for a quick kiss before whispering in my ear. "Let me teach you."

His words sent a cool shiver down the length of my spine and made my sweet spot ache for his body to fill me.

He reached down between us and wrapped his hand around my hand that already held his stiff dick.

"For me, I like it really, really tight." His voice was a mix of a whisper and a moan as he squeezed my fingers, tightening my grip around him.

A felt a fresh surge of energy flow into his boner, making it even harder than it had been before, which was something that I doubted was possible.

With his hand, he moved mine up the length of his dick, and I felt a small drop of cum seep out and lubricate my fingers.

Another moan escaped his lips as he made me stroke him faster and faster, until the pleasure overcame him, and he had to pull his hand away to steady himself over me.

I continued without him, a wave of pride flowing over me at the way he squirmed at my touch. I liked knowing that I was the one making him cower in pleasure.

Him, a mage so powerful who could command tornadoes and manipulate the air.

There he was, at my will. I controlled him just by a stroke of my hand, and that stroked my ego.

Opening myself up and letting my sexual energy run wild was freeing. I didn't know how I'd survived for as long as I did denying myself the simple pleasure.

"Oh my gods." He moaned as he squirmed. "I'd say you're a pro by now."

He smirked.

"Now it's my turn to make you feel good." With that he planted a kiss on my collarbone that made me shiver.

I had no idea that it was a sweet spot for me until his lips pressed up against it and it started to do devilish things to me, sending a tingling wave of passion to my clit.

It already ached, begging for attention, and Atlas was threatening to send me over the edge.

He trailed his kisses farther down, planting a row in the middle of my chest before bringing his lips to each one of my nipples, making sure to add a flick of his tongue at each stop.

I closed my eyes and succumbed to the pleasure that he was

handing out so freely, letting myself relax into the sensations.

After lingering over my breasts for a few moments to enjoy them completely, he continued his trail planting a kiss on my belly button and my panty line until his face reached between my legs.

Without a single word, he used his tongue to gently trace around my clit, being careful not to actually touch it.

An odd mixture of a moan and a groan erupted from me at his tease.

He looked up at me, making sure to lock his eyes on mine before taking two fingers and gently prying my tight hole open. By now it was already dripping wet, thanks to all the teasing he so freely gave. I inhaled quickly as I felt his fingers slide inside. I'd only ever had sex once before, and the only thing I ever used for my menstruation was a tampon, so his fingers were definitely a new experience.

I moaned at the pleasure of feeling myself stretch to fit him, and before I knew what was happening my hands found their way to my breasts and my fingertips were massaging my stiff nipples.

That mixed with Atlas' fingertips sliding over my G-spot was a match made in sexual heaven, and I bucked my hips against his hand in an attempt to get my clit in on the action. It felt so good that all I needed was a single second of clit stimulation to be sent over the edge.

Atlas looked at me with a smirk on his face.

"Hey, are you trying to cum on me?" He smiled.

"I'm so close." I whined.

"I know." Atlas half laughed. "Your body is like the wind. It's like it speaks to me, every nuance of your movement, every twitch of your muscles, the way your body squeezes around my fingers, they all tell me a story about what you need and where to take you."

He pulled his fingers from me and slid them into his mouth, sucking every drop of my juices off like it was frosting from his favorite cake.

"There's a reason I was avoiding that spot." He slowly crawled back over me, placing both hands just above my shoulders.

"Oh really? And why's that?" My confidence in my sexual abilities was slowly rising, enough for playful banter at least, so we were getting somewhere.

"Because I want to feel you cum on my dick."

His words nearly made me cum all on their own. I felt the head of his dick slowly push between my dripping wet lips and I opened my legs as wide as I could to beckon the monster inside.

I moaned and my face contorted into an odd expression of pleasure and pain.

I was right, he was a lot bigger than Apollo, and even Apollo was painful to welcome into my tight, untouched body.

"I'm sorry that I have to hurt you." Atlas pulled his dick all the way out and ran a finger over my cheek. "You're just so tight and new that your body needs to get used to me being inside."

I nodded, a single tear running down my cheek. It wasn't a tear of sadness, but just a reflex of my eyes watering at all the sensations.

He pulled me in for another kiss and just as our lips met, he thrust himself back inside, a little faster this time. He pulled out and did it again and again as we kissed and my body opened up to welcome him into the deepest parts of my body.

Atlas pulled away and looked into my eyes before picking up his pace, his body grinding against my clit and sending electric waves of pleasure exploding in my mind.

This was it, the moment that I'd been begging for. The moment my body has been screaming for. I was finally going to get a release to all the sexual pleasure that was rattling around in my body, ready to explode.

"I'm going to cum inside you. Is that okay?" Atlas asked, his voice shaky as he still thrust in and out of my tight hole.

I nodded quickly and he seized up, adding one final thrust deep inside of me. The head of his dick pushed into the farthest wall of my vagina and he tried to cram his entire beast inside. There was a warm gush as I felt him dump his load, and my body eagerly welcomed every drop of cum he was willing to give me. His pelvis pushed against my clit and it was just the right amount of stimulation to send me over the edge into an explosive orgasm. It was like every inch of my body vibrated and shook, a fresh wave of heat radiating off my body.

While I let myself give in to the explosive pleasure, Atlas quickly pulled out of me, holding his dick that had been scorched by the heat. I would have felt sorry for hurting him, but I was still too taken by the immense pleasure that vibrated throughout my whole body.

"Eden, you need to chill for a second."

Atlas' words fell on deaf ears as the pleasure hit its peak and an explosive ball of fire shot out from my body in a single burst. It was only when the fire was released that I came to my senses and opened my eyes in horror.

A wave of panic washed over me at the thought of burning the temple down. The ancestors would definitely not forgive that one.

I jumped up as the mystical ball of fire roared, ready to sprint to the manor butt naked to get Apollo to use his water magic to put it out, but the fire erupted and a mystical wave of wind swept through the temple.

"What heck is going on?" I screamed over the loud woosh.

I watched as the fire was mystically guided to the front of the altar and a flash of light nearly blinded me. The fireball was absorbed by the mystical shining gold chest— the same one that Apollo had said couldn't be opened.

After the flash of light, the room went still.

"What was that?" Atlas asked.

"I don't know." I mumbled, as I stared at the chest, its lid now opened wide.

Chapter Five

A wave of exhaustion immediately swept through my body, buckling my knees beneath my weight and sending me spiraling to the rough stone floor.

I screamed out in pain as the jagged rock cut into my soft flesh, sending jolts of electric pain up my legs.

Atlas scrambled to throw the blanket over my body and help me to my feet again just as Adler and Apollo burst through the front door of the temple.

"Are you guys okay?" Adler asked, slightly winded from the sprint from the manor. "The entire building started shaking and there was this burst of energy coming from–" His words trailed off as his eyes landed on Atlas' naked body.

He looked from Atlas, to me, back to Atlas.

A full few seconds had passed before Atlas realized that he was completely naked, with his anaconda on full display. He was so concerned with making sure that I wasn't hurt badly that he completely lost all of his reflexes for self-preservation until it was too late.

He jumped backward, scrambling to cover his junk, but the damage had already been done. Apollo raised a knowing brow at us, and shifted his gaze from me, to the altar that sat at the front of the room. His eyes immediately locked on the golden chest with its lid ajar.

"How the hell did you open that?" He asked with an urgency in his voice.

"Yes, I'm okay. Thank you for asking." I huffed.

I didn't know quite what I was expecting his reaction to be, but it involved a tad more jealousy and a bit more alarm.

Once again Apollo found a way to walk the fine line of my last nerve, and now it was an even more dangerous game to play.

I couldn't put my finger on it, but something about Apollo seemed to get under my skin more now. It was like his being just agitated mine in a way that it hadn't before.

"Good to know." Apollo spat the words back at me. "Now tell me how you got that thing open."

This time his words were laced with more panic and less sarcasm than they usually were.

Something about the situation didn't sit right with me anymore, not judging by the look on his face.

"I don't know!" I answered so quickly that my words almost ran together to form a single unintelligible one. "I just... You know... I"

I couldn't bring myself to say the words in front of all three of them. All of them together made me even more nervous than they did when they were apart.

"She climaxed, and an explosion of fire just erupted from her. We would have both been fried if it wasn't for whatever the hell is in that chest absorbing her fire magic." Atlas' tone was calm, but I could tell that inside he was probably more shaken by the events than I was.

He was sweet for stepping in for me, though. I looked up at him and offered half of a shy smile as a silent thank you.

He threw one back to me, and I nearly got lost lingering on his perfect dimples again.

Focus Eden, focus! I scolded myself. *What the heck did you break this time?*

I internally kicked myself for once again destroying something. I just hoped that this time it didn't result in the annihilation of an entire city.

Don't get me wrong, I didn't regret what had happened. I didn't think I was in the wrong, and I honestly didn't care what happened to Jade and Asher.

I just wished that an entire city didn't have to be reduced to ash to satisfy my karmic needs for revenge.

The angry fire simmered inside of me again at the thought of the whole ordeal, my emotions only fanned its flames.

I would have been lying if I said that my new thirst for revenge didn't throw up a few red flags in my brain. The old Eden wouldn't have dared execute a plan for revenge, and burning an entire city to the ground would have completely obliterated her sense of self-worth.

But I wasn't the old Eden anymore, and the smoldering fire magic that nearly burned a hole in my chest worked as a good buffer for my normal emotions making their way to my heart.

"Why are you so worried about it?" I asked. I realized the second that they left my mouth that the words sounded slightly more agitated than I had meant for them to, but there was no taking them back now.

And it felt kind of good to throw some attitude into the room for a change. It was about time that someone gave Apollo a run for his money, and thanks to the fire magic I felt like I could keep up for a sprint or two.

"Well, I'm sorry that I'm the only one concerned that an ancient, very mysterious, very *sealed* artifact has suddenly opened and I'm the only one concerned about what it might be inside." Apollo huffed and his hands clenched tightly at his sides.

Once again Apollo found a way to inch his way into the deepest cracks of annoyance that I had and dig himself a home to stay in.

Beneath my skin the threat of the ferocious fire magic buzzed as Apollo pushed me closer to snapping.

"Fine. If you're so concerned about what's inside the damn

thing, why don't I show you?" I was shocked at the words coming out of my own mouth. It felt like I hadn't said them, but something inside of me took the wheel and said them for me.

With that, I dropped the blanket to the ground, a cool wave of air rolling over my bare curves.

Adler's jaw nearly hit the floor at the sight of me naked, and even Apollo looked taken aback by my sudden rush of bold behavior.

But he wasn't the only one.

For a few split seconds it felt like I wasn't the only one inside my head. Like there was something else crammed in there with me, and that something was vicious. It was made up of a potent anger that threatened to destroy anything that got in its way.

I flounced across the room, sure to let the natural swing of my bare hips be accentuated just enough to command the attention of every guy in my presence. It felt like I was strutting an invisible catwalk. One with completely naked models, and half with water witches staring on angrily.

Without a single word I walked up to the chest, ignoring the magnificent golden shimmer that it gave off.

For a split second it nearly captivated me— the real me. But that was gone in a flash as the warm anger occupying my mind fought me to get control back.

"You wanted to see what was inside, so here it is." I said before throwing the lid back, opening it all the way and sending it clunking into the rough stone wall behind it.

Inside sat an old alarm clock, painted the same shimmering

golden hue of the chest was. It was the kind that still needed to be wound and held two silver bells at the top.

A laugh escaped my lips at the irony. I didn't know who had been trying to open it, or how long they put in the effort for, but if I were them I would have felt incredibly stupid. Imagine working for days, weeks, or even years to open a mysterious chest to only find an old alarm clock.

Talk about anti-climactic.

And a small part of me relished in the fact that was how Apollo was going to feel too the second I told him. He made such a fuss, like the world was going to end, for an alarm clock?

I spun around with a smirk on my lips. I shifted the weight of my naked body, still amazed that the embarrassment of having the most secret parts of my body being on full display hadn't hit me yet.

Armed with a single hand on my hip and a smirk that was enough to wipe the one off of Apollo's lips, I sighed.

"Do you want the good news or the bad news first?" I raised a brow.

Apollo groaned and rolled his eyes.

Atlas was still scrambling to get re-clothed, and Adler was still having difficulty picking his jaw up from the floor and clearing the stars in his eyes.

"The good news is there's only a dusty old alarm clock inside." I half chuckled as the words made their way from my mouth into the stale, dust-filled air. "That's also the bad news. So Apollo, you made a big fuss for absolutely nothing. Yikes." I shrugged nonchalantly, trying to hang onto every single drop of satisfaction that I got from rubbing Apollo's nose in the fact that I was right and he was wrong.

It was something that not a lot of people had the courage to do to him I guessed, judging by the pale shade of red that slowly seeped into his normally cool skin tone.

For added effect I reached into the chest and pulled the clock from its depths, holding it high and proud for Apollo to feast his eyes on. I'd found that visual representations of defeat tend to sting a little more.

If it were up to me I would have stood in front of the guys, gloating my win and flaunting my nude curves for as long as the thing inside of me held the reins, but my happy times were quickly interrupted by a low sound of rumbling that exploded from behind me.

"What the h–" I was blown back by an intense burst of magical energy that was released from inside the chest in a single pulse.

I clung to the alarm clock with everything I had, waiting for the harsh sting of the stone floor to tear into the flesh of my back too, but instead I landed on a soft cushion like substance.

I peeked out of a single eye, and quickly saw what had caught me was a mixture of each of the guys' magic. They'd all used it to interweave a hybrid bed for me to land on— even Apollo.

Suddenly it felt like the steaming anger had retreated from the controls in my mind, giving me back my body.

A twinge of regret reverberated through my body at how intensely I had gloated.

I looked up just in time to see a huge beast explode from the chest in the form of a giant bird.

It wasn't like a normal bird, it was more like the shimmering outline of one, colored in by what looked like a black hole dazzled with stars. Like someone had just copy and pasted a photo of outer space to fit inside the shape of a bird.

"What the hell is that thing?" I screamed over the loud rush of magic escaping from the box.

"That would be what I was afraid of." Apollo grumbled.

Chapter Six

The huge shimmering apparition exploded from the treasure chest and spread its large wings before jumping and barreling through the air straight for the door. I braced myself for the crash, holding my breath and waiting for it to either annihilate the dilapidated stones that made up the wall or kill itself trying.

But I was surprised to see it phase through the wall like a superhero or something, its outstretched wings only growing bigger as it sailed toward its outdoor freedom.

Apollo, Adler and Atlas all dropped to the ground, careful not to let it touch them.

I, on the other hand, still stood stupidly in the corner of the room, surviving the swoop of its swift wingspan by luck and luck alone.

"Holy shit." Adler said, his normally relaxed tone now tightly wound as the words spilled from his lips.

"It's real. It's actually real." Atlas had an odd smile stuck to the front of that gorgeous face of his. It was a mixture of surprise and excitement.

Apollo held a look on his face that was even more sour than the one he normally sported— and that was hard to do. I'd always wondered if it took a lot of energy to walk around everywhere like he had a stick shoved up his ass.

"We should have known." Apollo grumbled, before slamming the palm of his hand to his forehead.

"Hello? Is anyone going to care enough to fill me in?" I said, another toxic wave of anger simmering beneath the surface. It was like my fire magic was always there, lurking in the shadows hungrily awaiting even the slightest spark of emotion to use to rekindle its power that rested inside me.

"How were we supposed to know it wasn't a legend?" Adler argued, all three ignoring my comment, which didn't bode well for the looming threat of my fire magic.

"Because nothing is ever a legend, is it? They all come from somewhere. We were stupid." Apollo said, with his own signature brand of angry flare thrown in for a little seasoning to his words.

I opened my mouth, an equally angry rebuttal eager to spill from my lips, when I was cut off by a deafening screech that sounded from outside the temple walls. It was unlike any noise I'd ever heard in my life. A mix between a human voice, and an animal call, all blended perfectly into a pristine, eardrum-shattering pitch.

The guys all exchanged worried glances, again neither one even thinking to glance in my direction.

I didn't know why it made me so upset that they weren't acknowledging me. Deep down I understood why, there was a freaking mysterious being outside, and we didn't know if it was friend or foe. It was only logical to acknowledge that problem first, putting my feelings on the back burner. But even so, there was a twinge of unfamiliar jealousy that jolted through my body in red hot spurts.

Since when did I become the type of person who liked to be the center of attention?

I huffed silently inside my head.

Since you realized that you deserved it.

An unfamiliar voice answered quietly between my ears and I jumped.

Luckily I was able to blame the momentary involuntary muscle movement on the, still ear- shattering, screech that sounded from outside, but that didn't curb the intense wave of anxiety that flowed through my body.

What the hell was that? Was this it? The moment where I actually officially slip off the fine line that I'd been walking for a while and make the plunge into the dark, deep abyss that is insanity?

The guys rushed outside, trying to all file through the doorway to the temple at once, nearly getting caught at the broad shoulders.

I pulled myself from my thoughts and back into the intense reality that lay before me, pushing my ever-fading insanity to the back of my list of urgent things that needed my attention.

After all, a freak monster made of the stars would make it to the top of anyone's list, even with their degree of insanity excluded from the equation.

I sprinted after the guys, but only after snatching the blanket from the ground and once again wrapping it up. What was left of it after the second flaming incident was only enough to barely cling to the curves of my body. It definitely wasn't something that I'd wear for a night on the town, but for hunting down a mysterious creature it would have to do. It wasn't like I had much time to press pause on the upcoming battle to run inside for a wardrobe change.

But just for future reference, I made sure to make the mental note that running dramatically out of a building without a single article of clothing in my possession was probably something that I shouldn't make a habit out of on a regular basis.

Noted.

I scrambled out into the yard, the soft blades of grass tickling my feet as I ran until I caught up with the guys where they stood, perched between the temple and the creature, with the manor lying on the other side of its shimmering body.

Out in the sunlight, its form glittered even more, and I could truly appreciate the detail of every star and constellation it was made up of.

If I wasn't so unsure of what it wanted, or if it was even a friend, I probably could have spent all day exploring its beautiful essence.

But I didn't know what it was, or why it was there, so I'd have to spend time getting to know its outer shell some other time.

It let out another deafening screech, but it was even louder this time without the rough stone walls of the temple to soften the blow. The sound alone was enough to send all three guys spiraling to the ground on their knees, each clasping their hands over their ears and gritting their teeth so tightly that the muscles in their jaws bulged slightly. The looks on their faces were rabid, like the sound itself was going to either kill them or drive them mad. I couldn't tell exactly which one it was.

Maybe both.

The sound was uncomfortable, yes, and it made me nearly want to claw my eardrums out myself, but it wasn't as debilitating as they made it out to be. There they were, three of the strongest, most powerful elemental mages in existence, and each of them cowered at their knees while I stood tall.

Normally that kind of thing would make me feel uncomfortable— standing out from the crowd so much. I would have instantly been overwhelmed by the pressure of just knowing I was different from the rest, but something deep inside of me wasn't surprised, or intimidated, or even overwhelmed.

No, it was the same feeling that floated around my mind earlier that quietly whispered inside my head.

They're right to bow to you. The voice slurred its words ever so slightly that it almost reminded me of a snake. I couldn't tell right then whose voice it was. It seemed familiar. Like I almost couldn't put my finger on it or quell the nagging feeling that gnawed at the pit of my stomach that was currently occupied tying itself into enough knots to impress a sailor.

You hear them. You're the one with the power here, look at them cower. The voice lingered on the last word, making sure to draw it out into an entire breath.

That was when it hit me.

The voice wasn't someone else's voice at all— it was me.

"What are you doing inside my head?!" I screamed out loud at the beast, sure that it was the source of the oddities playing out inside my brain.

It had to have something to do with the chest that was opened or the temple itself. I didn't know, and I didn't even need to.

All I knew was that I wasn't the only one inside my head, and that realization alone was enough to send an uneasy feeling spiraling deep into my soul.

I wasn't alone inside the dark abyss that I called my mind, and that was the scariest thing to happen to me that day, even counting the shimmering beast that now hovered in the air, steadying itself with a few powerful flaps of its wings.

It wasn't like there was anything inside my head that I had to hide. I didn't have any deep dark secrets or some hidden agendas that could be compromised by someone else poking around inside there, but it was the simple principle of the fact that you would assume that your mind is the one place that you're safe from the judgment of someone else.

But how the heck was it even happening?

The bird let out a final screech, this one emanating a wave of aggression. The entire feel of the air around us shifted to one that was heavily charged.

The sound was enough to jolt me back to reality, and I tabled the strange voice in my head once again giving it a back seat to the problem at hand.

One perk to the creature having such a good set of lungs was that I was ninety-nine percent sure that none of the guys had actually heard my miniature meltdown, which was good. I needed time to gather my thoughts before I presented the mystical issue to them.

My eyes quickly darted to the guys as my heartbeat began to slowly pick up the pace. They were in the same spot, but they had devolved from the place they were at on their knees, to now lying in the fetal position on their sides, anxiously clawing at their ears.

It looked like I was the last hope. I was the only chance that they had to making it out of the predicament that *I* put them in.

How sad for them.

My lack of confidence didn't surprise me, but it did however anger the mysterious version of Eden that sat in my head, waiting to bark angry things at me.

I felt my skin start to tingle, and a feeling of pins and needles started at the base of my wrists and slowly clawed its way up my arms.

I took a deep breath and forced my heart to do the same, slowing the ferocious rhythm that it drummed inside my chest cavity.

My eyes darted from the guys on the ground, to the giant star-filled creature, and back again. Out of the corner of my eye I saw the creature's wings outstretch as it prepared to launch an attack on its prey while they still lay writhing on the ground with their ears covered.

The creature attacked fast, and to be honest I had absolutely no idea what kind of magic it possessed. We had already covered all four types of magic, and as far as my knowledge went that was the only kind that existed.

Nevertheless, I couldn't just stand there and watch the guys die, especially not after all the times that they had saved my sorry behind even when they didn't have to. The least I could do was return the favor.

Without giving it the full string of thought that I should have, I immediately jumped into action using the magical skills that they had taught me in our brief training time. I leaped out front and wackily inhaled, calling to the magic of air to wield with my fingertips. Nature happily obliged and a small spinning tornado of wind formed beneath my feet every time they got close to touching the ground, forming a hopscotch style tornado obstacle course that led directly into the battle. I stopped in the perfect middle between the two, surprised that I'd managed to make it there as fast as I did and just as the creature's wings struck up, I held my hand up. The pins and needles feeling still stuck, but this time I used it to my advantage, using every particle in my body to will the energy to flow from my hand and conjure something, anything that would protect us from whatever was about to happen. I shut my eyes tightly, my arms raised above my head when there was a loud thud. I opened my eyes to see a barrier made of a mixture of all four elements that I had commanded, all working together to form a magical shield.

A smirk came across my face and I felt the angry voice inside of me smirk too, because it meant she was right.

With a single push I threw my magic backward and it collided into the creature sending it into the air above our heads before exploding like a bomb. An intense pulse of magical energy flew out in all directions like a gust of wind, washing everything it touched in its power and raining shimmering glitter down on us. In the middle of the yard where the creature sat, a small piece of rolled-up paper quietly floated to the ground before making its home in the grass.

"What the hell was that?" I asked as the guys slowly emerged, wiping thin trails of blood from the sides of their faces.

Apollo turned to me with the most serious look on his face. "That was the guardian of the fifth element— the guardian of time."

Chapter Seven

"The guardian of what?" I blinked viciously at Apollo, trying to make sure I'd heard him correctly. Because according to every story, and every history book in the country there were only four elements. FOUR.

Five was unheard of.

It was impossible.

Wasn't it?

I'd found that the more time went by, the more possible the impossible felt for me.

There was a flurry of emotions running through me, far too many to sort through and unpack all at once. So I decided to start with the very beginning.

"Explain." My voice sounded a lot firmer than I'd intended it to, even for addressing Apollo who usually required some sort of backbone to be dealt with.

It was an accident, but it did the trick, because even Apollo straightened his posture and cleared his throat to dive into the details instead of dancing around the subject with a delicate mix of passive aggressive sarcasm like he normally did.

I held back a smirk at the effect that I'd had on him. I would have been lying if I said that having a backbone didn't feel good sometimes. I didn't know what it was about activating my fire magic, but something about it had seemed to unlock the aggressive assertiveness that I'd hardly been able to tap in before any of this went down. I kind of liked the rush of *I don't give a crap* energy that was new to my system. It was just the refresher I needed, when handling Apollo at least. And for that it was a lot less of a hassle than normal.

Adler and Atlas had finally made their way up from the ground and wiped away at the dried blood on their faces too.

Apollo glanced around nervously and for a split second I noticed a glimmer of anxiety in his normally harsh facial expression. He scanned the tree line quickly, and I watched his icy blue pupils dart back and forth from shadow to shadow that extended from the dense forest.

"Let's go inside first." He said, his voice suddenly a low hum. It was almost hard to hear because of how much base it normally held, but I made do translating inside my head. "We have no idea what that gust of magic really was. For all we knew it could have been some sort of mystical homing beacon."

Apollo's comments made sense to me, but judging by the way both of the other guys' eyebrows furrowed, I was the only one.

They both shrugged anyway, despite their silent and mysterious denial of Apollo's words.

I still clung to the tattered blanket, almost positive that after the last wave of magic made its way through the cloth, it was destroyed enough to at least be giving them a slight peep show, but I didn't even care anymore as another wave of exhaustion swept through my body quickly, threatening to sweep my own legs out from underneath me just as fast.

I nodded, and as the guys made their way up to the manor, still trying to pull themselves from whatever haze the magic had thrown them into, I sprinted for whatever the creature had dropped before it exploded.

Lying among the vibrant green grass, there was a rolled-up piece of yellowed paper. It reminded me of something that you'd see in an old pirate film, rolled up tightly just to get in the neck of an old bottle.

I could tell that it was aged pretty decently by the way it crunched beneath my hand, making me rethink the amount of force I used to cling to it tightly.

I couldn't tell if I was imagining it or not, but I could have sworn that I felt the familiar hum of some sort of magic running through the paper too. It was a feeling that I was slowly becoming better and better at identifying.

I didn't know that magic could be infused into paper. I thought curiously.

There's a lot that you don't know. The strange voice in my head snaked the words as quickly as I had. *But you will.*

I nearly tripped over my own feet at the sound of the voice. My cheeks began to blaze a bright shade of pink and I fumbled to recover, hoping that none of the guys had noticed my instant change in demeanor.

I had gotten lucky once with them not hearing my strange outburst, but I doubted that I would have such a stroke of luck twice in the same day.

If you can count a mystical creature nearly making them all deaf, and therefore being impossible for them to hear my outburst, luck.

I sure wasn't completely on that one.

The guys had already started on the journey back into the house before I'd even had the paper in my hand, so they were a good distance ahead of me already. I didn't mind though, after everything that had happened it was nice to walk by myself and take a few seconds to make sure I was getting all my deep breathing in.

I didn't even care if I had a nip slip in the beaten-up cloth that didn't even deserve the title of a blanket anymore. All I wanted was a few minutes to let myself actually settle down. I realized that I hadn't gotten that in so long that I almost didn't know what the heck it felt like anymore.

Who knew getting attacked by the freaking guardian of time

could take so much out of you?

Also, who the hell knew the guardian of time was an actual thing?

I guess I had to hand it to being an eden, I really learned new things on a daily basis being the only witch alive who could manipulate more than one element at a time.

Sure it was a pain in the butt most of the time, but I found myself desperate to find *something* to hang on to about it. I needed to find a single positive aspect, even if it was as small as my hopes and aspirations, and hang on to it for dear life.

Because people need to believe in something, especially when the world around them is crumbling to nothing but a pile of rubble in front of their eyes.

The house was quiet as I snuck back into the kitchen. Part of me felt a little uneasy at the complete lack of water spectre cooks scrambling about inside the space, but I chalked it up to arising nerves at yet another mystical foe emerging from the shadows.

Once again, I found myself looking for something funny to fixate on. My brain needed the smallest breadcrumb to focus on, something to grasp for the next few days to give me the extra push to keep doing what I needed to.

At least I don't have to worry about giving the staff a free show. I joked inside my head, the echo of it bouncing around again and again.

What's wrong with giving them a free peak anyway?

I flinched at the sudden materialization of the voice once again.

I clenched my fists tightly, the shock leaving my system quickly, only to be replaced with a wave of anger at the annoying persistence of whatever the hell had infiltrated the walls of my mind.

Was this a parlor trick that one of the guys had learned how to do?

Or maybe a way for Apollo to finally convince me that I was off my walker?

No matter what the source, the truth of the matter was that it was getting quite ridiculous and I would have liked nothing more than it to end at just that, sparing me from the need to stand up for myself yet again.

But does it even count as standing up for yourself if you're defending yourself from yourself?

I didn't know. It was confusing, and every second that I wasted was another second closer to the exhaustion clawing its way into my being and becoming a permanent part of me, and that was the exact opposite of what I needed.

I ignored the comment inside my head, deciding that if I did that it would certainly go away and there would be one less creepy, likely paranormal, issue that I had to deal with.

I begrudgingly trudged up the stairs, still yet to see a single person in the hallways.

Maybe the day was turning around, maybe there was still some potential to recover it. But it all hinged on me welcoming the scalding hot embrace of a bath, and it would have preferably ended with me on the couch already taking a nap, trying to charge up my social batteries before trying to put two and two together to solve a freaking magical mystery.

I made my way to the suite where I stayed, the half charred one, but that was an issue to deal with at a later time.

The minute I walked inside and closed the door I welcomed the warm comfort of solitude.

No matter how powerful of a witch I became, I couldn't help but go back to my roots. I was a loner by default, and even three steamy, sexy, completely head over heels elementals wasn't going to change that. I enjoyed the peace that came with being alone. It was when my mind was able to do its best work, including problem-solving.

And I could tell just by the vibe that I got off of the rolled-up piece of paper that we had one hell of a problem that was practically begging for me to solve it.

I made my way across the room and slid into the bathroom, a sigh of relief escaping my lungs at the site of the vintage bathtub, equipped with the tarnished legs and all.

I turned on the silver faucet and a gush of cool water spouted out and collected in the tub. I looked at it mesmerized by the rushing pattern of the waves it created. I'd never been someone who knew deep inside that they connected with a certain element. Even living with the water witches, I never shared their divinity for all things aquatic.

But I never felt that way about any other elements either. I found things to enjoy in all of the different factions because they all truly held traits to be admired.

Inside my hand the paper sat crumpled, my curiosity nearly burning a hole in my hand.

But at the same time, I was so freaking exhausted that it was hard to keep my mind on a single thing for long. I knew by the show of theatrics that whatever secret information the paper held, it was going to be dramatic. It was going to be a major revolution that would probably change my entire life yet again— it was obvious.

And I was never one to ignore the obvious.

Those were the exact reasons why I held off on opening it. My body needed time to rest, and I needed time to process what the heck was even going on. It was one thing after another, after another.

When was a girl supposed to find time to bathe?!

I finally let the tattered blanket drop to the floor, a sense of relief coming with it. It felt good to release it, throw it away with the wind and let my body be free in its most natural form.

I threw a splash of bubble bath into the water and watched as it mixed, slowly adding a froth of bubbles to sit at the top.

I stuck one toe in, and nearly moaned in pleasure at the perfectly steamy water. It had been so long since I'd actually taken a minute to enjoy something so small and simple, and it felt good.

I slid all the way down into the water until my back rested comfortably against the porcelain of the tub.

"Mmmm. Yes." I closed my eyes and moaned, letting the muscles in my neck relax gently and resting my head on the back edge of the tub.

"Oh, make that noise again." Apollo's voice came from across the room and made me jump.

I opened my eyes to see him perched in the doorway, his shirt already on the ground, revealing his carved abs.

I looked him over, from his feet to his head, mentally devouring every delicious drop of angst that oozed from his perfect skin.

"Did you miss me?" Apollo smirked.

Here we go again.

Chapter Eight

A pollo stood in the doorway with a tantalizing grin spread across his face.

"Is there something I can help you with?" I raised a brow sarcastically. "Or is it just a new habit of yours to burst into rooms when I'm otherwise occupied?"

I poked fun at his discovering me and Atlas. I thought it was hilarious, but the way his smirk slightly drooped and the territorial look that glistened in his eye told me that he didn't quite share my sense of humor.

I wished I could have said I was surprised, but I couldn't. Apollo had always stricken me like the little kid at daycare who didn't like to share his toys.

I was hardly a toy, and I was even more so hardly his, but still, the connection between us was undeniable.

But what did that have to do with him showing up in the doorway of my bathroom uninvited?

"The guys took up all the other bathrooms." Apollo wiggled out of his pants, leaving them in a crumpled heap on the ground.

I immediately ripped my eyes from the perfection of his bare body and pretended to be particularly interested in the water stain that blemished the otherwise pristine ceiling above me.

It was oblong and thick. It was only a few seconds before my mind made the connection of how much it looked like a penis, and my mind was brought back to Apollo's nude presence that filled the room.

Once again, I couldn't shake the inner goddess that screamed for sex. It felt like my legs were Pandora's Box, and once they were opened a calamity of sexual desires came tumbling out and refused to go back into the solitude of their hiding place.

I made the mistake of letting my eyes fall back on Apollo for a split second, and the ferocious hunger returned to its home between my legs.

Apollo was tall, and he seemed even taller towering over the bathtub.

His eyes lingered on my face, probably because it was the only thing showing above the sea of bubbles that were adrift in the water.

"Why don't you take a picture? It would last longer." I said before shifting my gaze away from his, awkwardly inspecting the painting that clung to the wall across the room.

I relished in my comment for a second, feeling like I'd chosen the perfect rebuttal judging by the thick silence that settled over the room afterward.

That was, until I felt a rush of cool air hit my chest, making my nipples instantly harden at the change.

What the–

I shifted my gaze back to the tub and watched as the water receded quickly, exposing more and more of my body as it disappeared. It gathered in a large orb suspended in the air just above the bathtub. It caught the light just right and cast an aquatic blue light over Apollo's face, with a glimmer of a faded rainbow here and there.

"What are you doing?" I scowled, trying to pretend that I didn't get wet at the realization of the lengths he would go to see my naked body.

He was determined, I'd give him that.

"Taking a mental picture, for later use." He winked before dropping the water back into the tub.

The intense shift in temperature was enough to make me jolt, and at that point my nipples didn't know what the hell was even going on anymore.

"Oh yeah? Two can play at that game." I smiled confidently before closing my eyes and taking a deep breath.

I tried to slow my mind and listen to the magic that coursed through my veins. A fraction of the tingling magic that I'd felt before crawled its way down my arms and I was able to lift a small orb, the size of Apollo's fist, before letting it drop back into the water and send a ripple of waves through the normally still water.

I groaned, frustrated at my lack of control of my abilities.

"That was cute." Apollo smiled devilishly before dipping a toe in the water and jumping back at the temperature. "Holy shit! Why do you have it scalding hot?"

I shrugged, holding in a giggle at his reaction. "Practicing for my place in hell I guess."

This time it was me who had the devilish grin.

I had to admit, watching Apollo make a fool of himself did make me feel a lot better about the crap show that my life was turning into.

Apollo went all in, immersing his entire foot into the water. He inhaled sharply, and his face went white, but his expression had *FUCK IT* written all over it, and he quickly lowered his body into the water at the opposite end of the tub.

He let out all the air he was holding hostage in his lungs, and way quicker than humanly possible his facial tone went from ghost white to nearly devil red.

I raised a brow at him, more seductively than sarcastically this time.

Inside the fire magic roared, and the feeling returned. The one that made me feel like I wasn't the only one inside my head.

The magical mixture was filled with red-hot lust, and it hit my veins all at the same time.

Suddenly my ego got a huge, sexy stroke. I actually liked seeing Apollo squirm. Big bad Apollo, who wanted me to believe he wasn't scared of a thing.

But something told me that after seeing me as comfortable as ever in practically boiling water, he knew I wasn't someone he wanted to mess with.

I let my eyes close gently and tipped my head back, once again resting it on the back of the bathtub.

The tub was wide enough to fit both of us inside, but in order for him to fit properly he had to weave his legs in the middle of mine. I felt him tuck his legs through, each foot resting comfortably perched between my hips and the smooth porcelain.

With one swift move he pressed his legs against mine, spreading them wide, sending a rush of warm water against my clit.

"Ah, much better." Apollo sighed, finally growing comfortable with the temperature.

Not accustomed, but comfortable.

"So, you and Atlas, huh?" Apollo leaned his head back, trying to mimic my relaxed pose.

"What's it to you? Isn't there enough Eden to go around?"

The words fell from my lips with a seductive drawl, and I wasn't even entirely sure that I was the one who had said them.

Well, of course it was me, but was it *me?*

It was so hard to be sure of things with the pesky magic infiltrating my thoughts.

"Of course there's enough to go around, but is there enough for me?" Apollo looked at me with a hungry gaze. I could feel it blazing holes into my skin without even opening my eyes. His voice was nearly a low, primal growl that did something terrible to the space between my legs.

Before I knew it, I found myself sinking my teeth into my bottom lip, and the hungry look that was in his eyes had made its way to mine.

"We're just going to have to see about that, aren't we?"

I didn't even know what I was saying anymore. It was like instinct was taking over, or maybe it was the magic, by that time the entire thing was just a sex-crazed, lust-filled blur.

Beneath my skin, the familiar sizzle of magic swam like a shark stalking deep waters, waiting for the first thing to jump at.

Looking for something to devour.

And there Apollo sat looking like a snack.

I latched my fingers tightly around the smooth walls of the tub, clinging to the edge so tightly that my fingers quickly grew sore.

I thought I was doing good. I swore I had it under control, but it seemed like with every second that passed the water between us gradually got hotter and hotter.

I held on, and put up a good fight, but then Apollo had to go and open his big stupid mouth.

I didn't know quite what he said because I was so focused on the way his soft lips looked when he said it. A single note of his gruff voice was enough to send me over the edge, and I quickly stood up.

Apollo's eyes grew wide, simply because he'd obviously thought his little escapade wasn't going to amount to anything.

I was sure he was poking a lion that he thought was asleep— but it wasn't.

And there he sat in its sights, waiting to become its prey.

I stood in front of him, staring down past my bare features.

Around us water sloshed out of the bathtub and splashed against the old tile floor, but regardless, my eyes stayed glued to him. I watched as the look in his eyes slowly progressed from confusion to understanding. Beneath the water, my eyes caught sight of his rock-hard member, practically begging for as much attention as my body was.

I watched the fire return to Apollo's eyes. The way he reached up and wrapped his fingers around my wrists only awoke my arousal even more.

With his hands around them firmly, he yanked me down and into his lap, with another round of water splashing out onto the ground.

Oh boy, here I go again.

Chapter Nine

Before I even made it all the way into his lap my lips found his, pressing tightly against them. I could feel the buzz of magic underneath his soft skin. There was an aura of lust that hung in the air around him, and I could feel my body feeding off his sexual energy. I inhaled it, letting it wash over the innermost parts of my body, leaving a layer of sexual desire behind.

"I knew there was enough for me." Apollo said when he pulled away, sinking his perfect straight teeth into his bottom lip.

"Oh honey, that was never the question. The question is, is there enough of *you* for *me?*" Once again the thing inside of me took over, holding my actions hostage as well as my words.

But I didn't care because of the euphoric feeling that spread inside of my head. There was no better feeling in the world than Apollo's fingertips brushing against my skin, and the heat of the warm water only had my senses even more piqued.

I grasped the back of his head and pulled him in for another kiss, letting my hands roam his body. They slide from his head, down his back, before sneaking their way between our two bodies and roaming over his prominent abs.

I delighted in the way his body shivered beneath my fingers, a single touch sending ripples of pleasure through his skin.

I wondered if this was what it was like for everyone, or if it was our fated spark that made sex with the guys so freaking amazing.

Either way, I didn't know how I had survived as long as I had without it.

A world without them, and a world without sex both seemed so far in the past, so disconnected from who I was then.

If it was what sex was like for everyone, I could hardly blame Jade for betraying me for it.

I'd betray me for it too.

It was a high that I'd never felt before, one that I was sure I was slowly becoming addicted to.

I sunk my teeth into Apollo's bottom lip and his eyes sprang open, surprised at the mix of pleasure and pain.

He hadn't expected it from me, but I was a fast learner— and boy was Atlas a good teacher.

The more I allowed myself to lean into my sexual urges, the

more my instinct uncovered inside of me. I grew more comfortable in letting go of my inhibitions and taking my pleasure to the next level.

Luckily for Apollo, my pleasure included his too.

As soon as my teeth clamped down on his lip, I brushed my hand against his dick, gently enough to get his attention, but not firm enough to give him anything more than a tease.

He squirmed, and all it did was to put a smile on my face.

I felt his fingertips find their place between my legs and massage my aching clit. My lips parted and a soft gasp escaped from them.

Apollo knew what he was doing to me, it wasn't his first rodeo.

But it wasn't mine either anymore.

I pulled him back in for a kiss and wrapped my fingers around him, and a fresh pulse of energy coursed through him, stiffening him even more.

I felt two of his fingertips part my lips and slide inside, sending an explosion of hot pleasure through my body.

I stroked him slowly, soaking in every inch of his fingers.

"What the hell happened to you?" He asked, his words coming out as a half moan.

"What do you mean?" The question caught me off guard and pulled me out of the moment.

I pulled my hand away from his dick and sat up straight, putting more space between us.

Something inside me bubbled up. I couldn't tell if it was anger, or confusion, maybe even sadness.

A confused look spread to Apollo's face.

"I just mean, you seem different than the first time. Not bad, just— different."

Anger rose up inside of me. I didn't know why, he was only saying what I'd been feeling but was too afraid to admit out loud.

I stood up, a semi-permanent scowl stuck to my face darkening my features.

I reached for a towel and wrapped it tightly around my body, feeling good about denying Apollo another glimpse of my body.

I huffed in his direction before stepping out of the tub, ready to give the meanest case of the cold shoulder that I had ever given. The second my foot hit the wet tile I remembered how carelessly I'd sloshed water outside of the bathtub, but it was too late and I lost my footing, sliding across the slick tile and onto my back.

An explosion of pain erupted in the back of my head as it hit the floor in a solid thud.

Apollo jumped from the tub, still completely naked. In one quick motion as fast as his feet hit the floor he used his magic to raise every drop of water from the tile and return it to the bathtub, leaving the floor completely dry.

"Are you okay?" he reached out a hand.

"I'm fine." I slapped his hand away, biting back tears.

"You're not fine, Eden. You almost cracked your skull open." Apollo thrust his hand in my direction again, this time telling me he was going to help me instead of asking.

"I said I'm fine!" I yelled.

An anger crept up my throat that was so hot it hurt, and the skin of my arms burst into flames. The fire magic was hot behind my eyes too. I couldn't tell if the magic had blurred my vision or if it was the tears that clung to my eyes.

I grit my teeth at the searing pain, and my body locked up.

"Eden, you need to chill out!" Apollo demanded.

But his demands only made the angry fire blaze even hotter.

He shook his head at the sight of the towel that clung to my body sparking up in flames, and the skin of my chest and stomach following suit.

He shook his head like he was disappointed in me, and the next thing I knew, an orb of water hovered over me for a split second before exploding and showering droplets all over my body, putting the fires out.

I rolled over and coughed hysterically, trying to expel the water from my lungs. Every inch of my body was thrown into a new type of pain, the shock of the two elements colliding.

I looked down at my arms just in time to see them harden a dark shade of black, like lava when it cooled, with only a few cracks rippling through it.

I felt like I was frozen, momentarily paralyzed by the rock clinging to my skin. It took nearly all my strength to bust my arms loose from its grip, and I watched the black chunks of soot fall to the ground before peeling the bits from the rest of my body.

"What is this stuff?" I asked, wincing at the pain of it ripping from my skin.

"Exactly what you think it is." Apollo said quietly. "It's what happens when our two elements meet. When fire magic meets water magic you get this."

He gestured toward me vaguely.

I took a second to focus on breathing, making sure my lungs weren't completely tarnished, and hoping way too hard that the black rock didn't form inside my lungs too, because then I'd be done for.

I sat on the floor, far too exhausted to get up.

"So..." Apollo's words trailed off like he was expecting me to say something.

"So?" I cocked my head to the side. I knew what he wanted from me, but I wanted to make him work for it. He was going to have to ask.

"So." The word came out like a statement this time, falling heavily on my ears.

I felt the angry magic simmer once again, but my skin still ached. I didn't think I had the energy to take on any more burns, so I tried my hardest to stuff it back into its cage.

It was a challenge. It was like Apollo purposely rubbed me in all the wrong places.

Maybe he got off on making me mad, I don't know.

Or maybe I hated that his sarcastic self was right.

There was something different about me, and not in a good way.

The old Eden might have had a lot of flaws, but her patience wasn't one of them.

Now I felt like a raging monster, one that even I didn't recognize. The smallest things set me off, but most of them had to do with Apollo, even more than normal this time.

"So." I repeated, knowing that my lack of communication would make him angry.

I didn't care.

His lack of communication made *me* angry.

So we might as well have sat there fuming.

Apollo sighed, and a saddened look graced his handsome features— a crack in the cocky, know-it-all, sarcastic armor that he always chose to wear.

Part of me wanted to ask him what was wrong because I really did care about him deep down.

But that part was being held hostage by the flaming anger that had taken over my mind. It was being held for ransom, and I wasn't willing to pay it.

Without saying a single word, Apollo grabbed a towel, ripped it from the hook that it hung on and wrapped it around his waist before turning to leave the bathroom.

Again there was a sliver of me that wanted so badly to shout at him not to go. To look into those icy blue eyes of his and ask him to tell me what was really going on in his head.

But that was part of the old Eden— what was left of her. And the old Eden didn't even come close to being as powerful as I was now.

So I sat quietly on the floor.

He slammed the door behind him, sending a wave of vibrations through the floor and all that was left behind was a cold, quiet, damp room.

As soon as Apollo crossed the threshold of the door, I felt the anger inside of me subside. It was like it came out just for him, and when he was gone it had done its job, so it could retire back into the recesses of my mind.

I didn't understand what it was about him that rubbed me so heinously. Sure he was cocky, and a know-it-all, and his handsome face could get a little annoying when combined with the other two traits but the only thing that had really changed was my fire magic being activated.

I groaned.

All of this was just more stress added to my freakshow of a life.

You couldn't make this stuff up. It was like a curse of bad luck followed me wherever I went.

I was so sick of it.

I wished I could just start it all over from the beginning, knowing what I know now would have changed everything.

I pulled myself from the floor and made my way to my suite, sure to grab the crinkled paper when I left.

I tossed it on the worn down, vintage dresser that sat against the far wall and slid a pair of plain black jeans and a black T-shirt on.

Before all of this, I wasn't the type of person who felt comfortable in all black. My life was unfortunate, but it wasn't *that* dark.

But now the color felt like it fit me perfectly.

Dark, just like my soul felt inside.

I reached for my brush and just as my hand swiped over the crinkled ball of paper, I noticed a glimmer of light coming from inside the folds in the mirror that lay on top of the dresser.

"What the heck?" I swiped a dark lock of hair from my face to make sure I wasn't seeing things.

It looked perfectly normal once again, until I reached over it. From inside a faint glow of yellow light emerged.

I grabbed the paper and opened it excitedly, hoping that whatever was inscribed on it could lead me to some answers.

My stomach sank into my shoes when I realized the paper was blank.

I'm not crazy. I tried to convince myself, but the odds weren't looking too good for my plea for sanity.

I cocked my head to the side and set the paper back down on the dresser.

I started to run a brush through my course brown hair, when my eyes flitted to the mirror.

A smile spread across my face.

I knew I wasn't completely insane.

Slightly? Maybe.

But completely?

Not yet.

In the reflection of the mirror a series of glowing scribbles traced across the paper, only visible in the reflection.

"Whoever made this was one smart bastard." I said out loud, growing more and more comfortable throwing swear words into my sentences that would have made the old Eden cringe.

Before I had a chance to examine the reflection to make sense of the markings, the front door to my room swung open and Atlas and Adler burst through it without a single knock.

"Eden you need to see this!" They both said, practically falling over one another to get through the doorway.

"You guys need to see *this!*" I held the paper out like a prize.

"Ours is more important." Adler said, his words stinging slightly.

"I doubt that." I said with a sure smile.

Atlas shifted his gaze, with a hint of worry in his normally soft gray eyes. "Don't."

Chapter Ten

My heart sank at the grave expression that mulled across Atlas' normally soft features. It would take the entire world collapsing on its own demise to cloud the spark in his warm eyes, but there he stood, his eyes as cloudy as an April afternoon.

Adler didn't look too hopeful either, his eyes nearly bulged out of his head.

I knew whatever had happened, it had to be big.

My eyes searched frantically behind them, part of me hoping that Apollo would poke his head through the doorway with his nearly permanent frown plastered to his face. At least it looked natural on him.

Natural enough anyway.

I sighed, clearly outnumbered by the two crazed balls of testosterone in front of me. Carefully, I folded the paper into a small triangle and slid it into my pocket, cautious not to be as careless as I had been before.

Not now that I knew there was something mystical hidden deep inside its mundane borders.

I took a step forward, but I must not have been moving fast enough because in unison both of their arms reached out at lightning speed and latched onto my wrists, pulling me forward into the hall.

I had no idea what was going on, but if it was enough to make both of them as distraught as they were, it was enough to raise a flag of alarm inside of me.

My mind raced, trying to think of what it could be.

But I couldn't think of a single thing because my life was already crazy as it is.

A fire-wielding psycho who also happened to be one of my four fated partners?

Couldn't make that up.

Me being the only mage in current existence to carry the burden of all four elements?

Couldn't make that up either.

Whatever was coming next, one thing was certain.

I couldn't make it up.

As they anxiously pulled me through the hallway, I couldn't help but notice the grasp of both their hands on my wrists, and the way it felt to have both of their skin touch mine at the same time.

Stop it, Eden.

I tried to pull myself from my dirty thoughts, but yanking my mind out of the newfound gutter that it called home was a lot harder than I'd thought it would be.

It was so damn comfortable. I felt like I belonged.

"Are you seeing this?" Adler turned and our eyes met.

His brows furrowed with worry, but I was still having a hard time shaking the sexy things crawling around in my head.

It wasn't until we passed the laundry room that I started to pick up on the oddities happening around us.

We rushed by it for a split second, but it was enough time for me to notice the huddle of water specters maids standing perfectly still in the doorway, one with a towel only half folded, holding it in the air.

It struck me as odd, taking that much time to complete such a small task. But it wasn't until we made our way into the kitchen that my stomach lurched to a halt, just like everything around us did.

"What. The. Hell." The words fell from my lips but they nearly got caught in the stale air.

A heaviness filled the room and I gulped, taking the scene in all at once.

The entire kitchen was filled with workers like it normally was, all still working on making a meal I'd finally eat, no doubt.

But what left a sour taste in my mouth was the fact that the room was as still as ice.

Just like the maids in the laundry room, every water specters in the kitchen stood frozen in place. Some chopped vegetables, others stocked the fridge. It didn't matter the task they were completing; they were all stuck.

Adler looked at me out of the corner of his eye, the hint of a smirk fresh on his lips at the swear words flowing more and more freely from my mouth every time.

I ignored his shock because I had shock of my own to deal with. "What is all of this?"

I would have turned to face the guys, but I couldn't bring myself to rip my eyes from the scene.

It was so strange to see time stand nearly still for someone else, while my own kept ticking away like it always had.

"What happened to them?" I asked, slowly approaching the head cook and waving my hand in front of his face.

I had to be sure that this wasn't one big, coordinated prank.

That was the last and only logical explanation that I could bring my mind to produce.

But it flew out the window the second the cook didn't flinch at my movement.

My next thought was that the spell that my ancestors had used to bring the specters to life, in all their shimmering aquatic glory, must have had a shelf life. Maybe that was why they all seemed to shut down, but the probability of the timing of that didn't give me much confidence in the theory.

"We don't know– but–" Adler started to speak but his words

were cut off almost immediately by Apollo's gruff voice.

"Does anyone know why every clock I walk past is completely frozen?" He walked into the kitchen with his tight-fitting T-shirt only halfway over his head and my eyes immediately snapped to his abs.

I forced my gaze away from his body, trying to focus on the matter at hand.

There was something mystically fishy going on, and I was going to get to the bottom of it, even if it killed me.

"This is some next level, freaky stuff man." Adler reached for the sandwich that sat on the plate in front of the cook and sunk his teeth into it.

"Really dude?" Atlas cocked his head to the side.

"What? It didn't look like he was going to get to it too soon." A muffled laugh managed to slip its way out of his mouth full of bread.

I zoned out their words, letting them fade into the background.

Nothing made sense. The clocks were frozen, the people were frozen, but why weren't we?

What made us so special?

And what could have possibly had the magic to do something like this?

Unless...

"What about the creature?" I asked, seemingly interrupting a petty argument over stolen sandwiches.

All of their gazes turned to lock onto me.

"What about the creature?" I said again, this time with more confidence weaved into the words. "You said something about a fifth element— the element of time, right? What if that's what caused this?"

"Okay, but why all of this? It doesn't make sense." Apollo asked, actively trying to avoid any eye contact.

"Nothing makes sense nowadays, especially not this. But it's what my gut is telling me, and if I've learned anything over the past few days it's to trust it more often."

The room fell silent and suddenly I had three pairs of handsome, peering eyes locked onto me, waiting for the next words to fall from my lips.

Being the center of all their attention at once made me squirm. I had to admit, it didn't feel nice to have their eyes locked on my body, and even nicer to see they were hanging on every word I said.

I pulled the piece of paper from my pocket carefully unfolding it and presenting it to them.

"It's blank, sweetie." Adler said with a smidge of sarcasm in his voice before ripping off another piece of his sandwich with his teeth.

"That's what I thought too." I scrambled to find something reflective in the kitchen, settling on a silver serving plate. Its reflection was so clear and unblemished that I could have used it as a mirror if I'd wanted to.

I held the stiff paper up, sure to angle the plate just right so that its reflection was clear to all the guys.

A silent sigh of relief escaped my lips when the glowing, mystical writing appeared.

It's good to know I wasn't crazy and just imagining it.

All three of them inched closer, huddling in around the silver serving plate, squinting to try to make out the lines that splashed across the page in mystical glowing ink.

"You're a freaking genius." Adler said, before yet another bite of his sandwich. "But what does it mean?"

I sunk my teeth into my bottom lip, deliberating for a second— letting my mind put the pieces together. I hadn't really gotten a chance to think about what it meant before they'd burst into the room and drug me down the hallway.

My eyes skimmed over the lines in the reflection of the platter, tracing them as they went. It was sort of like a mind game, trying to imagine them facing the right way, trying to figure out if they were backward in the reflection or whoever had written them had intended them to look that way. There were a lot of moving pieces in the mystery that I was trying to piece together.

I caught my mind wandering back to the past edens, and what they would have done.

They probably would have known right away.

For a split second I wondered if I was failing at the one thing I was born to do.

But I remembered what I'd just said— I needed to listen to my gut more. I needed to stop cutting myself down every chance I got because the world was already far too eager to do that for me. Why would I take time out of my day to make it easier for it?

I took a deep breath and cleared my mind. I had so many negative thoughts about myself and the world around me, that they cluttered up my mind. Of course I had trouble listening to my gut, it was no wonder. All the negativity was so loud inside my head I couldn't even hear myself think, let alone listen to my intuition.

I exhaled and imagined all the pent-up negativity that rattled around inside of me being blown out of my mouth like a cloud of black smoke. I exhaled until there was nothing left to expel from my lungs, and immediately felt lighter inside, like there was more room for the things that mattered— the things that were important.

I actively listened for my intuition, that gut feeling I knew I had at my disposal, just never truly respected like I should have.

When I opened my eyes again, I saw three pairs staring back at me like I was crazy, but I didn't even mind at that point.

It was like I saw everything in a new light— it's crazy how much my own anxiety was clouding my perception of the world around me.

My eyes traced the glowing lines once again. Every contour and shape was placed strategically, it was apparent to me now. It wasn't a jumble of lines and squiggles like a child would draw, there was a purpose and intent to each one. I just had to figure out what it was.

"It's a map." The words fell from my lips before my brain even had time to comprehend that I'd said them.

It was an odd feeling, much like the feeling I got when I was close to losing control— like something else was taking over and guiding my words. Only this time its presence didn't seem menacing, and it didn't carry with it the searing anger like the other one. This time it was a light, pleasant feeling.

More like guidance rather than a total loss of control.

And with it came a feeling of confidence in myself and my words.

A girl could get used to this feeling.

"A map of what?" Apollo asked with his arms crossed skeptically.

"Of the house."

Chapter Eleven

"How do you figure that out?" I could tell by the tone in his voice that Apollo was poking for a fight. Probably still bothered by what had happened earlier.

Before I would have overanalyzed the entire situation— his body language, the tone of his voice, the look on his face. I would have let it all get to me, found a way to make it all my fault, and internally tortured myself for it.

But the weight that I had released mentally was incredible. I wasn't sure exactly how it had worked, or why, but I wasn't going to question a good thing.

I thrust the paper and the platter into Atlas' hands, and he grabbed them from me, holding still with a questionable look on his face.

But Atlas was sweet, and for some reason he had more faith in me than I'd ever had in myself, so he didn't say a word.

And Adler was too busy trying to finish his food to be able to fit a single word out of his full mouth. I hurriedly made my way to the pristine white cabinets on the far side of the kitchen and took a moment to silently admire the shimmering golden doorknobs before snapping myself back to attention. I rummaged through the first cabinet, tearing its contents apart in search of a paper and pen, which I found lying at the bottom.

I made my way back to the guys, perching myself on the kitchen island and beckoning for Atlas. I re-drew the contents of the paper squiggle by squiggle until its pattern was duplicated in the dark black ink.

All three of them closed in, hovering over my shoulder to get a look at the page. I could feel Adler's warm breath brushing against the bare skin of my neck, and it sent a wave of shivers flowing through my body.

"It still looks like a bunch of random squiggles to me." He said, finished with his impromptu meal.

I looked down at the paper with my brows pulled tightly together. I chewed on the end of the pen nervously and I thought.

He was right, the markings still didn't make much sense. Even though I wished that I could have said that I knew, the truth was I had no idea what it was we were looking at.

I could feel the imminent trap of the negative thoughts threatening to slip back into the recesses of my mind and drag me down once again, but, armed with my recent wave of confidence, I fought back.

It was only when I'd forced the thoughts from the dark space inside my mind that I realized how much energy it took to hate myself all the time, and I wasn't going to waste that much energy again.

With that realization, there was a shift inside of me, somewhere far deeper than even I could reach. Like a magical switch being flipped at the epiphany, followed by a second wave of confidence, this one much fiercer than the last.

I recognized the small rush of magical energy that came with it. It was mixing itself with the hot, angry energy of my fire magic and creating a new magical cocktail inside my body. One that had spunk, and flooded my thoughts, bathing them in the magical high.

I got this. I gave myself a mental pep talk. *Someone made this puzzle; that means someone can solve it too.*

It was a different feeling, talking to myself positively, and I caught myself wishing that it could be like that all the time.

I stared at the paper so hard that my eyes started to dry out and I had to blink back a few times to keep the harsh, scratchy feeling at bay.

I rubbed at my eyes and tilted my head to the side, ready to throw in the towel and think of another way to solve it when I brought my gaze back to the page, and a hint of familiarity rushed over me.

"This is it." I smiled, twisting the paper to the side a few times, until the voice inside of me told me to stop.

The guys all exchanged confused looks with one another, trying to see if anyone else knew what the heck I was talking about.

I didn't care if any of them didn't get it because in my head it all started to make sense. The pieces were putting themselves together inside my mind.

I flipped the page over and squinted my eyes, carefully deciphering the faint marks where the pen's ink bled through and tracing over them darker.

I made sure to get every last line before holding it up proudly, revealing a small map of the property and a dotted line traveling through it.

"It was hard to piece together because it was sideways *and* backward, but I did it." A bright smile beamed from my face, proud at the work I'd done.

Atlas and Adler smiled too, not trying to hide their amazement.

It was Apollo who was still committed to looking like a human storm cloud, but I was determined not to let his energy infiltrate mine.

"Here's the house, here's the temple, over there is the forest, and back here is the creepy old well." I shuddered just thinking about it.

The more I pointed out the different landmarks, the easier it was for them to make out the sea of markings into an actual map like I could.

"How the hell did you figure that all out so fast?" Apollo's face started to soften a bit at the fact that he was impressed by me.

"I'm not completely sure." I said honestly. "It's like the lines just rearranged themselves inside my head to make the picture."

That was the easiest way I could think of explaining it.

Apollo nodded, like it was no surprise. "The eye of the eden." He pursed his lips tightly.

My lost expression must have given away the fact that I had no idea what that meant.

"It's an ability that the edens have that helps them see things that others can't. It's all part of guarding the elements."

I nodded.

There was obviously a lot that I had left to learn, and I would be the first to point it out. I was never one to act like I had all the answers because quite frankly I didn't have a freaking clue what was happening most of the time.

But I had the ambition to learn, and that had to count for something.

"Now the question is, what are you leading us to?" I directed the question toward the paper, like the inanimate object would speak up and tell me, but I knew there was only one way to get to the truth.

We were going to have to follow the markings on the map and see where we ended up. A huge part of me hoped that it wasn't marching us into the face of danger, but the track record for me walking into hazardous situations was too much to ignore, and I knew I'd have to march forward anyway, because Asher was still out there, doing god knows what, and don't even get me started on Jade.

Every time I thought about her, my skin crawled and the magic inside of me simmered below the surface, wanting to be released to wreak havoc.

I looked up from the page to see everyone staring at me, once again waiting for the next move.

Even Apollo bit his tongue, waiting to see what I had to say, which was new for him.

But I knew my time was dwindling. I had a small window of time before he gave up and tried to take charge himself, and my newfound confidence would shatter into a million pieces.

"First, we need to see how much is affected by–" I paused, trying to find a word that would even begin to describe whatever was happening inside the manor, but I drew a blank. "This." I said, hoping that summed up all the crap that had happened so far.

My eyes scanned the room until they fell on a radio that sat on the counter. I made my way to it and flipped the switch on, waiting to hear something— anything, but not a single sound played. There wasn't even any harsh static from a dead station, just silence.

A small red indicator light shone beside the power button, so I knew that it was working.

But the silence gave way for an uneasy feeling to creep up into the pit of my stomach, and it bubbled with nerves. The more I investigated the phenomenon, the more unnerving it became.

I remembered the old television that sat in the living room and pushed the doorway that separated the two rooms.

Surely there had to be some sort of clues somewhere.

"Eden, wait!" Adler called for me to stop, but it was too late. I'd already flicked the power button on, and a bright photo lit up the screen with hues of oranges and yellows.

My heart skipped a beat when I realized what I was looking at.

It was a still photo of a news broadcasting, the word *live* written in big red letters in the corner of the screen. I guessed by the slight blur that it had frozen in place, mid broadcast, on an image of Asher.

Pyromaniac Destroying Air Sector Main Square - Commander's Emergency Evacuating The Entire Sector

I read the bold headline. Then I read it again, and again, and again.

Whatever was happening, it didn't just freeze the entire manor, it froze the entire country at least, and maybe the entire world.

And to top it all off, I finally got an answer to the question that had been plaguing me— what was Asher up to?

It wasn't until I was about to shut the screen off that I noticed the small square in the bottom corner.

Water sector completely destroyed, thousands dead.

Inside the square was a photo of a huge crater in the ground taken from the sky.

That was it. That was what was left of the town that I grew up in, hell, the entire sector.

That was me— all me.

I immediately felt the rush of hot magic flood my mind and blur my conscience. I felt a sick sense of pride that I'd been powerful enough to blast a hole that big with my magic.

The same magic that bubbled inside of me at that very moment.

The hot stares of all three guys trickled across my skin.

I could feel their eyes staring me down, trying to gauge if I was at risk to put another crater in the earth or not, but the truth was that I felt surprisingly relaxed about it all.

The headline kind of made my stomach spin, but other than that, I had become numb to my transgression. The guilt no longer plagued me like it had earlier.

My main concerns were Asher and Jade.

Screwing me over and trying to take my life wasn't enough, they had to keep going?

"What does he want?" I asked.

All three guys jumped at my words, like they'd expected more action and less talking.

I turned to see the confusion in their faces as they still processed my words.

I raised a brow and waited for an answer.

"That– he–" Apollo tripped over his thoughts, always trying to be the first person to answer wasn't always the best.

"We don't know exactly." Atlas admitted. "To make everyone feel the pain he feels inside maybe?"

I turned to the television, my eyes locked on his glowing orange figure. He was poised on the top of a tall building with his arms stretched wide, two streams of fire spraying away from his body.

That didn't seem right. It didn't add up. What did making other people suffer do for his own pain?

"What do you think he wants?" Adler asked.

"I don't know. But I'm going to find out."

Chapter Twelve

❝ You're sure the first stop on the map was the front yard?" Apollo questioned.

I fought the urge to immediately groan.

He was clearly still upset with me and searching for ways to get under my skin. I didn't know what it was with him, but it felt like he liked it when I was out of control. He liked to push my buttons and then rush to "save" me when I exploded— literally.

It was one of the less desirable traits that he had, and I hadn't noticed it sooner. I was too busy overanalyzing every word that came out of my mouth, and trying to tiptoe around everyone.

Now, it was like the fire magic gave me the boldness to accept my flaws enough to be able to notice his.

"Yes, I am the one with the eye of eden, remember? Unless you've suddenly somehow learned how to command the other four elements now? In which case be my guest and feel free to grab the map and take charge."

I knew my words would cut, that was why I'd said them.

Apollo huffed at my comment.

"I think we should split up. We'd cover more ground that way." He said before grumbling something underneath his breath.

The only word I could make out of the slew was *temple,* before he sulked off in his typical Apollo brooding fashion.

Atlas looked at me and Adler.

"I'll go with him to make sure he doesn't break something." I could tell that Atlas wanted to roll his eyes, but he was far too sweet to do something malicious like that.

"Looks like it's just me and you." Adler winked, and I couldn't help but laugh.

He was the laid-back, funny one. The one who was always eating, even in the middle of a paranormal crisis.

Him trying to change lanes and be the sexy, serious one was too much for me to hold in.

But what I liked about Adler was that he laughed too. He didn't take himself too seriously, and his energy carried over to me.

I was glad that we were thrown together in the impromptu pair up, because when I was with him I never felt pressured to be an eden. I didn't feel like I had to flaunt my abilities, or always say the right thing. I didn't have to try too hard to be romantic, or even care what I looked like.

I could just be me.

My mind went back to the night we'd spent talking at the kitchen table when things had only moderately gone to crap.

That night, that conversation, was one of the few times that I'd had alone with Adler. It was short, but even then it gave me a glimpse of who he was— the type of person whom I wished I could be.

Care-free. Caring. Funny. He was the whole package, wrapped up in a tattooed, sexy package.

I raised a brow and started our work, searching through the bushes that sat in front of the house.

"You know he doesn't mean to be like that, right?" Adler joined my side, sifting through the flocks of roses.

Neither of us knew what exactly we were looking for, but when we found it, we would.

Or, that was the hope anyway.

"Oh really? He could have fooled me." I raised a brow.

"He's a lot to handle, and he lays it on pretty thick."

I'd say.

"But he really likes you. I've never seen him look that way at someone before. Not even Daya."

My interest perked at the foreign name, and I tried to keep it from showing but Adler picked up on it instantly.

"Shit, he didn't tell you about her?"

A slight smirk curled my lips at the forbidden information. It was too late to turn back. Adler was in a corner and he knew it.

"He's going to hate me."

"He already hates *me.*" I rebutted. "So talk."

Adler wrestled with himself for a moment, trying to gauge his chance at surviving me or surviving Apollo, no doubt. I was half flattered when he opened his mouth to spill the beans, confirming that he thought his chances at surviving an Apollo attack were better than surviving mine.

"This was a long time ago." He started. "I want you to remember that. A long, long time ago before we were put to sleep."

I pretended to be overly occupied with the bushes, but the truth was that they weren't giving me much to go on, and my interest had been taken elsewhere, eagerly anticipating what was going to come from Adler's mouth next.

"Daya was Apollo's spark."

The statement hit me in the gut far harder than I'd expected it to.

I didn't know why the words hurt so much or why I felt sick when I thought about them, but I did.

I already knew that, contrary to popular belief, it was possible to have more than one spark. I was obviously a proof because I'd sparked four times. But what I couldn't figure out was why the thought of Apollo with anyone else made me ill.

He was an asshole, and I didn't even feel bad thinking that. Swear word and all, he was the king of assholes. But something told me that deep down, he had a heart of aquatic gold.

Maybe this Daya girl knew that too.

That thought nearly broke me too.

Adler eyed me cautiously, eagerly keeping an eye out for the first sign of flame so he could run, no doubt.

"Go on." I half laughed.

I liked the way he tiptoed around me. It was kind of cute.

"What happened to her?"

"She died." Adler said too quickly.

I looked up and the expression on his face told me that I'd finally found the one thing that made chill, laid-back Adler uncomfortable—death.

It was understandable. Even for someone as fun-loving and relaxed as him, death was a hard one to tackle.

There was a pain that flashed behind his eyes that told me there was more to the story about him and death, but I knew I could only wrestle one thing out of him at a time. And at that moment, getting to the bottom of why Apollo chose to be so sour was at the top of the list. I let him take as much time as he needed, getting up and brushing my hands against my pants.

These bushes were obviously a no-go, unless whatever the map had wanted us to find was a rotting bird's nest and some bugs. Even though I grew wary that the item might not even be in the bushes, I made my way to the row that sat on the opposite side of the front door, got to my knees, and started rummaging through the tangled, thorny mess once again.

Adler took some time to gather himself and moved to meet me before continuing.

"Sorry I just–"

I held up a hand, stopping him.

He didn't need to explain. He didn't owe me, or anyone else an explanation about why he felt the way he did.

It had taken me my entire life to figure out that simple truth, and now that I'd finally found it, I wasn't going to let go of it.

Adler nodded, understanding what I was saying, and a slight smile spread across his face.

God, he was cute when he smiled and his eyes almost closed entirely. His teeth were perfectly straight, and so white they could have blinded a horse.

Not to mention the tattoos that crawled down his neck, and the way their color somehow deepened in the sun.

He reached into the bush to search once again, and the carved muscles in his arm flexed beneath his skin.

A warm rush of energy blew past my skin as I realized just how off track I'd become.

I couldn't help it. I hadn't been alone enough with Adler to know how irresistible his personality made him. Sure he was handsome as all hell, but it was his personality that tied the knot.

And made me want to untie my pants.

A thorn pricked my finger and the pain was the perfect distraction that I needed to pull my mind from the gutter.

I cleared my throat nervously and shifted my weight, ignoring my panties in their wet glory.

"Daya. We were talking about Daya." I said, hurriedly breaking the silence and realizing how desperately awkward the words sounded.

Adler took a single look at me and chuckled. I couldn't tell if it was a *I know you want to rip my clothes off and ride me right here in the front yard* chuckle or not, but my cheeks reddened anyway.

Just to be safe, you know.

"Right. Daya." He cleared his throat before pulling his arm out of the bush, hopelessly empty just as I'd pulled mine out. "Daya was Asher's sister."

The plot thickens. I raised a brow as I hopelessly tried to put the pieces together inside my mind.

But even then, I still couldn't make sense.

Why was Asher so angry?

Why was Apollo so angry?

Why was *I* so angry?

So much anger, so little time.

"At first Daya and Apollo couldn't stand each other. That happens a lot with opposing elements, but fire and water mages in specific. It's like something in their DNA despises one another, like they're not compatible— doomed to despair."

Adler's voice was laced with a dramatic tone for effect.

Finally things started to make a little more sense for me.

No wonder I had woken up and wasn't able to even look at Apollo's handsome, cocky face without getting upset. It was like he found new ways to get underneath my skin without even trying.

"Then one day Asher got hurt, and Apollo came to the rescue. He used his water magic to lift and carry him more than three miles, all the way back to his home in the fire sector. After that it was like he changed in Daya's eyes, and they sparked."

Adler watched me closely, as I watched him.

He still had that look in his eye, like I might break at any moment and take the whole world down with me. It was both flattering and offending at the same time.

After he realized I didn't have any comments to add, he continued on.

"Everyone told them that it wouldn't work out. Fire and water have always been two signs notorious for not getting along, but he was lovestruck. Everything went smoothly until Daya's powers activated." The octave in his voice shifted, his tone gradually slipping into a darker drawl, very different from his laid-back, upbeat tone. "As you already know, fire is the most potent element there is. It does things to your brain, and your heart, that the other elements don't."

Part of me had wished that someone had filled me in on all this before my fire element had activated. I wished that I'd been even the slightest bit prepared, but even so I wouldn't have been able to stop myself from exploding.

It was destined to happen. I was slowly starting to see that.

"She wasn't herself, everyone could tell. The power is more potent in some people than others, and with it comes a steeper loss in sanity."

His words sent shivers down my spine and a sadness in my heart.

I was powerful enough to decimate an entire city. Did that mean my sanity was going to slip away from me as fast too?

"So?" I unconsciously leaned forward, waiting for the next words to leave his mouth. "What happened?"

Adler got to his feet, clearly done with his search of the rose bush. "No one knows for sure. They got into an argument one day, and Apollo followed her into the woods. A few minutes later there was an explosion and Apollo was the only one who came back, with his body covered in burns."

My heart hurt at the thought of Apollo's pain. He was a know-it-all, but I cared about him. There was no denying that, and I'd grown protective of the guys. They were the closest thing I had to a family.

Chapter Thirteen

A pollo in love with someone else. The thought alone was enough to make the fire magic inside of me simmer.

Adler could tell, it was written all over his face.

Having people fear me was something that I didn't know if I'd ever get used to.

The old Eden would have completely crossed the street to get out of someone's way out of fear of inconveniencing them. She'd take other people's crap without a word. She was everybody's doormat.

The new Eden burned towns and made the world's most powerful mages tiptoe around her like a bomb that could be detonated at any moment.

I didn't know what was worse. I went from one extreme to the next.

I took a deep breath and moved along the side of the house, only casually sifting through the bushes as I went. My gut told me that, whatever we were searching for, it wasn't there.

"You know you don't have to look at me like that." I said when I noticed the same look plastered across Adler's face.

"Like what?" Adler stuttered as he quickly tried to make himself look busily uninterested in me again.

I couldn't help but laugh. It was a genuine laugh, the kind that starts in the pit of your stomach and grows until you can't take it anymore and spit it out into the atmosphere.

The contagious kind.

Adler stared at me for a moment, baffled by how quick I could swap out my emotions before the contagion spread to him and he started laughing too.

He laughed so deeply that his eyes started to water, and tears streamed down his face. The sight was enough to keep fueling my laugh, and there we stood. We were gridlocked in a battle of laughs that had gone so far that neither of us was even making sound anymore. My eyes watered too, and with it came a dull ache in the muscles in my sides but I didn't care. It was a welcomed kind of pain, the kind that comes with a dose of happiness big enough to make it worth it.

I finally gave way and let myself fall to the ground, sprawling out on the soft green grass, my body still convulsing.

I was finally able to catch my breath, the laugh subsiding to a small chuckle now, and Adler collapsed into the grass beside me.

We both lay quietly after the laughing had stopped with frozen smiles on our faces, and I realized that even in times where the world seemed to be ending, I still found ways to be happy. I still found ways to smile, and that was something that I didn't know how to do before any of it started.

Before Asher showed up at the coffee shop, before Apollo learned exactly what nerves to work on me, before I'd even known Adler or Atlas, that would not have been possible.

I let people play with my emotions too much, and I let myself become addicted to what people thought of me. I was constantly caught up in how other people looked at me, that I didn't even know how I looked at myself— and that was the problem.

I let out a sigh and allowed myself to sit in the happy high that settled into my bones. It was a warm and fuzzy feeling that buzzed in my chest and spread to my aching cheeks.

Maybe it was fire magic, I don't know. All I knew was it was because of Adler.

He made me feel comfortable enough to allow myself to be happy, something that even I couldn't accomplish.

I turned to look at Adler with a smile still on my face and was surprised to see his eyes already locked on me with a look of admiration.

"What?" I said, the blood in my cheeks rushing to the surface.

"Nothing." Adler shook his head, his dark eyes still locked on mine. "You're just beautiful is all."

If I'd thought I was blushing before, the intense wave of heat that hit my cheeks after those words proved me wrong.

"No, I'm not." I turned and pretended that I was even more enamored by the white blobs of clouds that slowly cut through the sky.

"But you are."

I felt Adler's hand lie onto mine, and he weave his fingers between mine.

At first I shivered beneath his touch. It felt like it had been forever since someone had touched me like that, or maybe not ever.

It wasn't sexual, and it wasn't platonic.

It was just caring. And I needed a little bit of that at the moment

Adler was funny, he could make someone belly laugh for five minutes straight easily if he wanted, and that was despite the tattoos that crept up his neck and his slightly intimidating face.

But underneath that he was sweet too, and I couldn't help but wonder why.

What had happened to him in life that had made him come out just right, and I came out like— *this.*

"I'm not beautiful. I'm kind of a monster." I laughed the words out, but there wasn't a single thing funny about the way I felt about myself.

There wasn't sorrow or remorse in the words either, like you'd expect. They just came out as a coldly stated fact.

It was true. I could feel the magic inside of me morphing my thoughts. It grabbed a hold of them and twisted them into all different shapes until they turned dark and seething, just like the magic was.

I could feel my old self fading to the back, letting the magic walk all over her like she let everyone else do.

The truth was, I didn't feel beautiful. I felt like a monster, just like I said.

A low hum of sadness flowed through me, like a sad melody playing on repeat. It was there, but it was faint as I realized the longer I held the fire magic, the harder it was to feel anything other than anger and resentment.

The closest I felt to normal was when I had sex. It woke up parts of me that had been forced into hibernation, and for a minute I was me again.

But obviously I couldn't have sex forever— even if I wanted to.

I looked beside me to see Adler propped up on one elbow, with his cheek resting cushioned in his hand.

His dark eyes were locked onto me with a laser focus that made me squirm.

"When I was a baby, my parents left me on the steps of the earth temple."

He said the words slowly, like he had to make a decision about whether to let each one fall from his gorgeous, pink lips.

I raised a brow, genuinely shocked by his confession. Someone so happy, so laid-back, so fun, I would have never guessed that we shared the same trauma.

Although his was a lot longer ago than mine, I was sure the sting of abandonment felt the same.

"I'm–" I stuttered looking for the right words to say, also knowing that there weren't any. What words can you tell someone whose parents didn't want them enough to raise them? No matter how much time passes, there is always a piece of the little kid trapped inside, hurt and alone. No amount of elemental power fixes that.

I gave up on my search for the perfect sympathies and exhaled deeply.

"I don't know what to say."

"Shit sucks." Adler said with a grin.

"Yeah. Shit does suck." I said, my tongue effortlessly gliding over the word that I once wouldn't have dared to utter.

I searched his eyes for something, I just didn't know what it was. I almost got lost in his dark brown pools. For once I saw a look in them that I recognized from the mirror.

It must be the mark of all the lost children, the sting of being forgotten.

"I was taken in by the mages." He said, finally breaking the silence. "But for a long time, I was mad as hell about everything, just like you."

"Well, in my defense you also didn't have chaotic fire magic seeping through your veins."

"No, but the magic of being abandoned is pretty chaotic too."

His words hit me in a soft spot that I didn't even know I had.

"For a long time I felt like I didn't belong. I didn't earn my spot in the earth temple, and I wasn't born into a prominent earth mage family. I was abandoned on the steps. For the longest time I thought that was my only qualification, my misfortune became a core part of my destiny."

He gazed off at an unknown spot over my shoulder, but I could tell that he wasn't with me anymore. He was gone, somewhere far in the past. Somewhere he didn't think he'd travel to again anytime soon.

"How did you overcome it?" I caught myself leaning forward onto my own arm, nearly toppling over waiting for the next words to leave his lips.

"I realized that it wasn't the qualifications that other people gave me that made me worthy of the magic that I held. No amount of training, even in the temple, could teach someone the type of magic I have. We're all born with different degrees, no more, no less. It was the magic that chose me, even when my parents didn't."

His words hit me like a freight train and reminded me of something Atlas had said about the different types of magic and how they were living beings, not a force to be tamed.

They were a force to be chosen.

"Eden, you are literally the most powerful person on the planet, maybe even in existence, and that is being modest." His eyes were locked on mine now, and as much as I tried, I couldn't bring myself to tear my gaze away from his.

Not when he had tears collecting in the corner of his eyes. I couldn't do it.

I opened my mouth to protest but he brought a finger to my

mouth, pressing his soft skin against my lips.

"You are the only person alive who can control all four elements. Even now a fifth has popped up, something completely unheard of, and you know what? It wouldn't surprise me for a single second if you were able to control that one too. You know why? Because you're strong as hell. And you're a badass. You don't tell yourself that enough, so I will. I'll stand next to you every day and annoy the shit out of you with reminders if I have to. Because you're the most amazing person I've ever met, but you're also the most insecure and you deserve better than that."

I blinked back my shock, while my brain was trying to decide if I was warmed by his words or offended.

Maybe both.

Was that possible?

Adler slowly let his finger drop from my lips, his soft skin sliding against mine on the way down.

I felt something stir, the mixture of lust and fire magic, and like every other time I could feel it spiraling out of control fast.

I thought back to the explosion I'd released after I climaxed with Atlas, and the damage I could do again.

I sunk my teeth into my bottom lip, trying to fight my urges.

I ripped my eyes from Adler's and pretended to be interested in the lush blades of grass of the small patch that lay between us.

We were lying so close.

When did we get so close? Or hadn't I noticed it until now?

Adler slipped his hand beneath my chin, the touch of his against mine once again sending trickles of energy between my legs. He tilted my head up, forcing my gaze to meet his.

"Don't fight it. If you fight the magic, you let it win. Lean into it and make it your bitch."

That was it. I couldn't take it anymore. So I grabbed him by the collar of his shirt and pulled his lips to mine.

Chapter Fourteen

I didn't care that we were on the front lawn, out in the open. Time was frozen, it wasn't like someone was going to drive by and see me swallowing his tongue.

I couldn't help myself, the way his lips moved when he told me to give in was enough to drive any girl mad. My clit throbbed, begging for attention, and my panties slowly grew wetter as our lips met.

At first I could feel the surprise on his face when I took charge, his eyebrows raised high. But the longer my lips pressed against his, the more the muscled in his face softened and he too gave in to the urges he had.

I had felt an attraction to Adler ever since I laid eyes on him, he did spark with me after all. But his was a lot more slow-burning than the attraction I felt to Apollo and Atlas.

It wasn't any less, it was just softer around the edges and hot with passion in the middle. The kind of thing you want to take your time to feel out and enjoy every blissful second of it.

I took time to get to know the inside of Adler, and I couldn't wait until he got a chance to know my insides too.

All the best parts of my insides.

After a few seconds of making out I released his shirt and it fell, wrinkled, against his chest. I slowly brushed my fingertips over the tattooed skin of his neck, a wave of pleasure rushing through me as he shivered beneath my touch. I knew he could feel it too, the magical connection begging to be solidified by bringing our bodies together as one.

I didn't know if it was a spark thing, or if I was just the most turned on that I'd ever been, but I didn't care.

I was going to claim him as mine. I was going to let him shove himself into every hole that I had, and stuff me in every place that he would fit.

And when I was done, I was going to let him fill me with every ounce that he had. I didn't know if it was the fire magic that made me feel so possessive of him, or if that was just who I was now, but I wasn't going back.

He was mine now, and I didn't care if I had to have him fill me with cum over and over and over again to make him realize it.

I dragged my fingertips over his neck and rested my hand on the back of his head, tangling my fingers in his slick black hair, squeezing a fist full of it.

I was moving off instinct now. When he told me to lean into my urges, I listened and now it was all I could feel. My passion and lust scorched so brightly that I didn't think that I could feel anything else until I released it, preferably all over that gorgeous chiseled face of his, but the specifics weren't important.

With my fist full of his hair, I yanked his head back, forcing his gaze to the sky and leaving his neck wide open for me to do as I pleased with.

I brought my lips to his collarbone and planted a kiss there before clamping my lips and leaving a dark red hickey as a trail of where I'd been.

A gruff moan escaped his lips and out of the corner of my eye I saw his hand tighten to a fist, grasping a handful of grass and ripping it from the lawn.

So you do have a sweet spot.

I worked my way up the length of his collarbone, leaving dark red love marks behind and growing wetter every time I heard him moan. I finally made my way to his neck.

I didn't dare disgrace any of his skin ink with a hickey, not like you'd be able to see it underneath the dark black ink anyway, but I was sure to gently sink my teeth into his skin. I was driving him insane. I didn't need to feel his dick to know that it was rock hard. The sexual energy was basically oozing out of every pore in his skin. It radiated off of him like heat.

Nibbling on his neck was just the straw that broke the camel's back.

He used his weight to topple my already uneasy balance— it was hard to balance on a single arm and entice him at the same time.

I fell onto my back and before I even knew what was happening, he was on top of me, with a hand planted firmly next to both of my shoulders.

"I'm sorry, was I too much for you?" I flashed my puppy dog eyes sarcastically at him, but I knew my devilish smirk would give me away.

I wasn't sorry for a damn thing, and if I had a chance to do it over again, I'd bite him harder.

Adler leaned in and kissed me roughly. My bites had set the tone, and I was getting the vibe that he liked it harder anyway.

"Never." He said as he pulled away.

For once I looked up and saw a wave of mischief embedded in his dark eyes, paired with one of the sexiest smirks that I'd ever seen.

Sweet, laid-back Adler had a thing for rough sex. Who knew?

Then again, it was looking like sweet pushover Eden did too.

Who knew?

Apollo and Atlas handled me a lot differently than Adler did. They handled me like I was a fragile thing, so new to the world of sex.

Adler shoved his hand up my shirt like he didn't give a shit.

But it worked well for him because I knew he did.

It's all about balance.

I cooperated as he shimmied my T-shirt up and over my head, leaving me in my bra. He looked me up and down, like I was the most delicious meal that he wanted to devour, and I was prepared to let him taste every inch of me.

"You're even more beautiful with your shirt off." He said planting revenge kisses across my collar bone.

I waited for the jolt of a hickey, but it never came. He was surprisingly gentler than I'd expected, and it threw me off.

I looked down at him impatiently as he continued his love trail down past my belly button and stopped at the start of my pants.

He looked up at me, taking pleasure in the sexual frustration in my eyes.

"Oh, I'm sorry. Were you in a hurry?" He said, imitating the innocent puppy dog eyes that I'd flashed him earlier.

I half laughed and half groaned. Leave it to Adler to set me on fire with lust and then drag it out to be funny.

I hated him and loved him at the same time.

"Well, I kind of want to cum before I turn eighty."

"Then you're in luck. Time's frozen, remember? I have all the time in the world to test this sweet little cunt of yours." He said with the snap of my pants button.

The word was so dirty, so vulgar, that it made my skin crawl with sexual energy. I loved it more than I thought I would, and I would have paid him any amount of money to just say it over and over again in that smooth sexy voice of his. Hell, I would have cum to that alone.

There was a glint in his eye, he knew he had me right where he wanted me, and I had a feeling that he wasn't going to let me go anytime soon.

I tried to help him pull my pants down but the second my hand traveled to my nether region I felt the sharp pain of him slapping it away.

A rush of fresh warm blood flooded to my cheeks. I didn't know why him taking charge turned me on the way that it did, but I knew once I came, I'd never be able to look at him the same.

I started to wonder how the hell he was so good at hiding the dark, kinky side of him, but my mind got distracted when I felt him rip my pants out from under me in one fail swoop.

"What are you, a magician?" I laughed.

"The way I'm about to eat you out is going to be pretty magical." He didn't even give me a single second to process what he'd said before sliding my panties to the side and flicking my clit with his tongue as a preview of things to come.

Literally.

I squirmed, my mind flooded by the pleasure that erupted but it was short-lived as he pulled his face from between my legs and made his way back up to my lips.

He pulled me in for a kiss, making me taste myself on the tip of his tongue before pulling away and looking into my eyes.

"Just so you know how delicious you really are." He said,

brushing a long strand of hair away from my eyes.

I looked up at him, and I could have sworn that I felt another electric spark go off in my eyes.

He felt it too, I could tell by the shift in his gaze.

"Another spark? What the hell–" His words were cut off when I wrapped my hand around the back of his neck and forced his mouth back down to mine.

"Less talking, more fucking." I moaned in his ear, shocked by the low sexy tone of my own voice.

I hadn't even stuttered over the word this time, it felt natural falling from my lips.

In a split-second Adler had his pants and his shirt off.

He was driven so crazy that he didn't even bother taking off my bra or panties, he just pushed them aside to make room for the stiff cock that had been bulging inside of his pants.

I felt the droplets of precum smear all over my dripping wet lips as he rubbed the head of his dick up and down them, a look of satisfaction crossing his face when he felt me getting wet for him.

His dick was big, I could tell by how thick his head was.

How they had all been graced with elemental magic, and great dicks I didn't know, but I didn't want to question a good thing.

Without a single word, I felt him slowly start to push his dick in, stretching my tight opening just enough to fit him inside. He entered me slowly, but I didn't care. I wanted to feel every inch of him, and I wanted him to fill me. My body was his for the taking, and I was ready to get taken.

He got halfway in, inching slowly, before he thrust hard inside of me, making me yelp both in surprise and in a wave of pleasurable pain.

Before I had a chance to moan, he brought his lips to my ear, so closely that I could feel his warm breath up against the skin of my neck.

"I'm sorry, I'm going to need you to be as quiet as possible for me, baby girl. Can't have the guys walking in on me claiming you."

His words sent a shiver down my spine, but it was his hand clamped tightly over my mouth that sealed the deal for me. I melted, growing more wet around his dick than ever before. He pulled out and thrust into me a lot more roughly this time, and a muffled moan escaped my lips. Even the sound of my moans through his clamped hand turned me on.

He pulled out and thrust into me again, fucking me harder and faster each time. I had never been so perfectly claimed in my entire life. Apollo and Atlas couldn't hold a match to how rough Adler fucked me. By the third pump he had me convinced, it was a cunt. A kinky, soaking wet thing for him to stick his cock into.

And I'd never been happier about that in my life.

"God, you feel so fucking perfect inside baby girl." He moaned underneath his breath; the nickname alone was almost enough to make me cum.

He could sense I was close to going over the edge, probably by how loudly I moaned, even through the barrier of his hand.

Because in a single movement he pulled his dick out of me and flipped me over, putting me on all fours.

I felt his arm reach around me and his hand resume its place over my mouth before his cock slid back into my cunt from the back, gliding all the way in and grinding into the farthest walls of my pussy.

I moaned louder and louder as he fucked me doggy style, demising me to only my primal, instinctual need to fuck. I was so taken over by my lust that I didn't care how hard he fucked me, I needed release, and I was going to let him give it to me.

He fucked me harder and faster. If the muffled moans weren't loud enough for the guys to hear at the temple, the sound of his dick clapping my ass cheeks definitely was, but at that point he didn't care either.

I felt my body seize up as I was pushed over the edge of ecstasy, my pussy tightening around his cock. That was enough to send him into overdrive too and I felt a gush of warm cum flood into me, filling up every inch.

Adler panted for air before pulling out and collapsing naked in the grass.

"Holy shit. That was perfect." He said between heaves.

I soaked in the lingering feeling of pleasure that floated around.

I was about to say something, but I got distracted by a small mystical glimmer of light coming from an apple tree next to the house.

"Do you see that too?" I asked, nodding toward the tree.

"No way." Adler half laughed. "I guess that's what we've been looking for."

Chapter Fifteen

I'd never pulled my clothes on faster in my life than I did the second I saw the flash of light coming from the tree. I was sure it was the sun reflecting off of something lodged inside, but the question was, what the hell was it?

In the blink of an eye I was dressed again and barreling toward the tree before Adler even got a leg back into his pants.

The apple tree was a large one, and I was almost positive that I hadn't seen it before time froze. It was next to the house, in the middle of the walkway that led to the back of the house.

I was sure I had walked through it before on the night I spent roaming the property and found the secret tunnels.

But I was positive that I hadn't seen it.

It wasn't like other apple trees; it was one that would have left an impression. Its leaves were a fluorescent shade of pink, and the apples that clung to it were white.

"What the hell is wrong with this tree?" I mumbled.

The look of it mesmerized me. It was like the more I stared, the more interesting it got. I found myself fixated on one of the shining white apples, my gaze getting lost in it.

The more I looked at it, the more it looked like the reflection inside of it was moving, like a galaxy floating through space, its glittered particles whirling.

The apple was one of the low hanging ones, almost perfectly at eye level. Before I knew what I was doing, my hand shot out and I slowly made my way toward it, overcome by the urge to rip it from the tree and sink my teeth into its milky white goodness. It was unlike any apple I had ever seen before.

I just about brushed my fingertips against it when I felt Adler's hands clasp around my shoulders and yank me backward, out of arm's reach.

It was like I was jolted back into reality, amazed at what I'd almost done.

"A freaky pink apple tree appears out of thin air and your first instinct is to touch it?" Adler raised a brow, obviously questioning my sanity.

He was right too. It was a rookie mistake, and at that point I considered myself far past the rookie stage.

But still I couldn't help it. It was like my body was taken over by something else, and I knew what that felt like, thanks to personal experience.

I simply nodded. I couldn't even think of a word that would begin to explain what had just happened.

"Do you think we should go find the guys so we can figure out what to do with this?" He simply nodded in the tree's direction, knowing better than to look at it directly after what had just happened to me.

In theory it was a good idea, the more people we had, the better chance we had at figuring out what it was.

But one thing I'd learned was that real life didn't always add up to theory, and I was afraid the second we left its vicinity it would disappear.

And if one of us left the other to guard it, there was no doubt that whatever magical pull it held would rope us in; we'd grab an apple, and well, I had no idea what would happen after that.

That was the scary part, not having a single clue what was going on.

Adler read my expression and nodded.

"We're kind of fucked, aren't we." He said it like a statement rather than a question.

"That makes twice now." I said, holding in an inappropriate laugh.

Adler cracked a smile at my joke, and his shoulders rose and fell with the small chuckle he let out.

"You're getting there, just don't quit your day job to become a comedian just yet."

All jokes aside, we were in some deep shit, and I didn't even feel bad saying it.

I sunk my teeth into my bottom lip and gnawed at it as I weighed our options.

Suddenly I felt a jolt at the back of my head as something small and round collided with it.

What the–

I turned to see a shimmering white apple lying at my feet.

A wave of angry fire magic simmered beneath my skin and I clenched my fist, willing myself to get it under control.

I remembered what Adler had told me about not letting it control me, and instead leaning into the feelings that it gave me.

He was right, it seemed like it got more out of control when I fought it.

Embracing it was much easier and far more fatal for those around me.

So instead of holding the anger and the magic inside, I let it flow, my normally brown locks bursting into bright yellow flames.

Adler jumped back, his eyes wide, but he didn't say a word.

He was a smart guy, and he knew better than to talk when I was blowing off steam— err, fire.

I let the angry magic flow, my flaming hair whipping in all directions, until it slowly simmered to a stop, returning to my mundane brown locks.

"Alright. Now that we're all calm, I think it's time we figure out what the hell threw that." Adler approached me cautiously.

My eyes darted from the apple, to the tree and my heart skipped a beat when they locked on to someone perched on it.

It was a guy, and he lay on his back, balancing on a thick branch perfectly.

He had purple hair that framed his face, and nearly reached down to his clean-cut jaw. His eyes were closed and his face was relaxed, his arms dangling down off the branch and swaying back and forth.

He looked as comfortable and natural as ever in the tree, like an animal lazily resting.

I jumped back at the sight, started.

"Holy crap!"

My words spooked him enough to make him open his eyes and cock his head to the side at me.

Our eyes met, and for a second there was a glimmer of confusion in his deep purple irises.

"What? What is it?" Adler looked from the tree, to me, and back to the tree.

I raised a brow and gestured toward the tree.

Obviously there was no need to explain what was right in front of his eyes.

Right?

Adler looked at the tree again, confusion in his face.

My eyes shifted back to the guy. His interest was piqued enough for him to get up from his comfortable position. He now sat criss cross, balancing on the branch.

Even a branch as thick as that, I wondered how he kept himself perched up there.

His face was relaxed, but there was a mischievous smirk on his lips.

I watched him reach for another enticing apple, pluck it from the tree, and chuck it directly at us, hitting Adler in the back of the head this time. If freaky things weren't happening, it would have been hilarious, I give him that.

But I was too distracted by the fact that a mysterious, apple-throwing stranger was perched in the even more mysterious freaking tree.

"What the hell do you think you're doing?" I planted one hand on my hip and slanted my stance.

The second he heard my voice he froze, with a lock of purple hair still in his face.

His skin went completely white, and the once mischievous smirk on his lips fell to a look of shocked despair.

He looked over his shoulder, searching desperately for someone who wasn't there.

"Are you just going to sit there like you're stupid, or are you going to answer me when I'm talking to you?" I said, surprised by my own demanding tone.

"No!" He said in disbelief, a wide smile spreading across his lips. "No! You can see me?"

His voice was velvety smooth, and almost melodic as the words fell from his lips.

Adler's gaze shifted from me, to the tree, and back to me, his own look of disbelief embedded in them.

Before he could get a single word in, the other guys came rushing toward us, barreling as fast as they could. If I didn't know better I would have sworn they were children trying to race each other.

"Guys, some freaky shit is happening in the temple, we came to show–" Atlas' voice trailed off and his pace slowed as he saw me staring off into the abyss, Adler waving his hand in front of my face.

"What's her problem?" Apollo said, a hint of anger still lingering in his voice.

"Talking to invisible entities, you know, the usual for her." Adler shrugged sarcastically.

I would have hauled off and landed a punch square in his shoulder if I was in my right mind, but I could barely focus on their voices because the pull I felt toward the mystery guy was so great.

I had never seen anyone with hair such a deep shade of purple as his, and I'd definitely never seen anyone move the way he did. It was like he was weightless; he defied the laws of gravity the way he sat perched in the tree.

Everything about him was different, even down to the one-piece jumpsuit that he wore, almost completely made of dark leather. There was a V shape cut into the neck of it that plunged down far enough for me to get the most tantalizing peek at the finely carved muscles of his chest. He wore long black gloves that met the bottoms of his sleeves for a cohesive look. And to top it all off he had a small satchel hung across his chest.

It was something that wouldn't have even come close to working for anyone else, but somehow he pulled it off with the perfect amount of finesse.

He moved through the branches quickly and effortlessly. He reminded me of a cat, jumping from one to the other, or a monkey.

A sexy purple monkey.

Wait, what?

"By god, you can see me." He said with a slight curl of his lips just as his feet hit the ground.

It took me that long to realize that he had an accent. I couldn't tell if it was English or Irish. Maybe a hybrid of both. All it did was add to his mysterious charm.

"Of course, I can." I said matter-of-factly. I turned to the three stunned faces looking back at me like they thought I needed to be admitted to a psych ward immediately.

"Oh, come on! He's right there, standing right in front of you all!"

I thrust my hand out into the air in his direction, the smirk on his face starting to get on my nerves.

I saw now that he was tall and skinny, but in a muscular way. Maybe that was why he was so agile.

I couldn't help but look at his handsome face and wonder if he was that agile in bed.

Boy I bet that would be a ride. No pun intended.

I clenched my fists tightly.

Focus.

"I'm sorry love," His smooth voice glided across the light breeze that blew through. "But I'm afraid you're the only one who can see me." He shrugged his shoulder paired with a slight chuckle. "In fact, you're the only one who has been able to see me for a century."

There was a hint of surprise thrown in with his English accent, a combination that worked surprisingly well.

The guy's faces still looked at me like I was crazy, but I ignored them. There were more pressing matters than them questioning my sanity.

"You're the carrier, the mage of–" I paused trying to figure out how to phrase it.

"The mage of time, darling." He said with a grin, flashing his perfectly straight pearly whites. "And might I say, it's about time you found me."

Chapter Sixteen

Time. The mage of time, standing right in front of me, with a mischievous grin spread across his face.

I didn't know why I was so awestruck. The day before I had no idea that a mage of time even existed, let alone that he was so damn attractive, but there he stood in front of me, in all his violet sexiness.

"No way, did you just say the mage of time?" Adler said in disbelief.

"Are you sure she knows what she's talking about? Maybe you just fucked her silly." Apollo's tone walked a fine line between being spiteful and argumentative.

My cheeks immediately sizzled with a lukewarm magic that threatened to grow if I didn't get it under control.

Adler didn't know what to say, he'd already gone back to being the chill, laid-back version of himself, which meant that every ounce of spunk and fight inside of him had returned into its docile hiding place inside his mind.

"Ouch, that's harsh." The stranger tilted his head to the side, before throwing in, "But it's kind of true though. You two were kind of going at it like rabbits, right? It's not like I was watching purposely, but, you know, I couldn't help myself."

"Oh shove it!" I said, my angry magic exploding out of my mouth in a stream of fire like an angry dragon. "I'm nobody's property, okay? I don't have to choose. I have the right to fuck whoever I want, however hard I want to."

The fire in my breath simmered, and I felt a release of the strange onset of anger that had erupted inside of me.

My words were more geared toward the random stranger's cryptic judgment, but I had a feeling that they'd all interpreted that the message was meant for Apollo, which it kind of was, so I didn't bother trying to correct them.

"I found the mage of time." I huffed, finally turning to face all three of them head on. "He said I'm the only one that can see him because–" I trailed off, realizing I really didn't even know why either.

"Because I've been trapped in a time loop for the last century, well, more like banished but the devil's in the details you know?"

I rolled my eyes.

"Because he was stuck in some magical time loop for the last century."

The last century. That meant that they'd all been hidden away around the same time, but why?

I was about to ask him for more information when Atlas interrupted.

"That brings me to why we were barreling toward you in the first place." He finally was able to circle back. "We were in the temple, and there was a flash of light and a third carrier door appeared at the front of the altar. One that definitely wasn't there before."

This was no coincidence. I knew better than to believe that.

It was all connected, just like every other unfortunate event that took place in my life.

I rolled my eyes over to the stranger, with a tired look in my eyes.

He fake whistled and pretended not to notice my eyes burning holes in his perfectly unblemished skin.

"Talk, time boy." I said, noticing the way the others' eyes quickly darted to each other uneasily.

I didn't know what the hell it would take to convince them that I wasn't making the entire thing up. *Maybe a few more apples to the face would suffice as a decent wake-up call that I'm not insane.*

I thought.

But I let the thought drift off as fast as it had come.

"It's the entrance to the realm of time. It's what in the bloody hell trapped me in the first place." For a second there was a look of fear in his violet eyes. "It's the only way I can break the curse of being here, stuck between two realms, forgotten and alone."

His words were laced with sadness, and for once since I'd been ignited by my magic, I felt myself stepping into someone else's shoes.

I couldn't imagine being trapped in a magical place, tucked away in another world that only I could see.

It would be maddening to survive a few days in that hell, let alone a hundred years.

"The name's Silas by the way, since I'm sure you were aghast with worry about the handsome stranger in front of you." There was a glint in his eyes. Something about his accent roped me in and strapped me down to every word he said.

I would have gladly listened to him read a freaking grocery list.

"Silas Finley." He flashed his pearly whites and there it was.

The tingling in my eyes, the spark of magic.

"No, no, no, not another one." I groaned, my cheeks turning a shade of pink.

"Was that– Was that a spark?" He brought his hand up to his cheekbone and gently rested his fingertips there, trying to sort through what was going on.

"Unfortunately." I groaned. "Silas, the guys. The guys, Silas." I lazily introduced them, knowing fully well that the others couldn't even see him.

Everything going on was exhausting, and I was tempted to just quit. Time was frozen. I could have easily just lived at the manor forever, kept the world safe from Asher's reign.

It was a tempting option, and I nearly went for it until I felt the hot smolder of fire magic in the pit of my stomach and realized even if time was stopped and the world was safe from Asher's toxic magic, it wouldn't be safe from mine. Even with time slowed, the vicious magic inside me grew more and more out of control. Even with the things that I'd learned to try to control it, I could feel it slipping from my grasp.

How long did I have until I became Asher? Angry at a world that did nothing for me. How long until I detonated like a bomb again and took out countless people who were frozen in time, without a single chance to escape?

A battle raged inside of me, constantly shifting between having no remorse for destroying my hometown, and feeling like shit about it.

I tried not to wonder if there were any lives lost. I tried not to think about the childhood homes that were destroyed.

But there was a menacing little sliver of me buried deep inside that wished I could take it all back.

Wait a minute. I paused, a master plan brewing inside the thick skull of mine.

In front of me stood the mage of time. He could command the hands of the clock of life himself. He'd been trapped for a hundred years but didn't look a freaking day over twenty-five and I was the eden.

If he could control time, maybe I could too.

Maybe there was a way I could go back and fix everything.

Maybe there was a way I could keep myself from releasing the wild power that tried to claim my body as its own.

A way I could make it right.

I clenched my fists tightly, set on the plan.

I was going to fix it. I was going to fix everything.

***

"And you're sure it's safe to go through?" Atlas raised a brow at the shimmering golden door that had appeared at the front of the altar.

I glanced over at Silas, who sat perched on top of the shimmering golden chest, once again defying the laws of gravity.

He sat so nonchalant with one leg bent and his elbow resting on top of his knee. He shook his head slightly to move the strands of purple hair that nearly hung in his eyes to the side and smirked.

"Of course, it's safe. Do you think I would lead you astray, little mouse?" His lips curved at the edges and I ripped my gaze from his.

"He says yes." I directed to Atlas. "And don't call me little mouse." I spit the words in Silas' direction.

He found my spunk humorous. Maybe it was even a kink of his, I didn't know. But all I knew was that the way he looked at me confused every part of my body. It was like it melted me and aggravated me all at the same time.

I did feel like a mouse, set in the gaze of a sly cat who could pounce at any second.

"Never." He said with a hint of defiance on his tongue.

He had no problem throwing my spunk right back at me, but when he did, it was in a playful way, much different than Apollo's blatant anger.

"Inside the door you'll find yourself in the realm of time, the place that was once my home. If you can survive the maze in the garden and make it to the castle, you'll be able to retrieve the first half of the sand clock, and we'll be halfway to getting this party started!"

He clapped his hands together, like he didn't just casually say *if you can survive the maze in the garden.*

What the hell?

"The sand clock?" I asked, careful not to mention his words of survival. The last thing I needed was all of them stressed and at one another's throats.

We'd deal with any impending doom when we got to it, like we always did.

"Yes, the sand clock. It's the instrument that bestows the power to control time to the carriers. If you ever plan on hitting resume on your world, that's the remote you're going to need to do it with."

"Meaning, I could control the element too?" I made sure to clarify. I didn't want to get my hopes up and get my heart set on my master plan to correct the timeline only to get let down at the last minute and have my fire magic set off.

"That is, only if the element chooses you, beautiful."

Silas was clearly feeling the effects of the spark, the same ones that I fought with every ounce of might that I had.

One spark I could live with, maybe two or three, four was a stretch, but five was borderline unbelievable.

I had always been taught we only got one. One magical moment with your soulmate, the person you're going to spend forever with.

I was going on five.

It was hard to wrap my mind around the fact that the universe had paired me with five, insanely powerful and equally sexually blessed sparks.

Me.

The old me would have felt insecure, like I didn't deserve the attention.

I nodded and shifted my glance to the guys suddenly realizing that their eyes were all on me.

And instead of making me nervous, it gave me tingles in all the right places.

I didn't know how to quite explain it, it was like Silas' addition to the group brought us full circle. I didn't know we were even missing anyone until the zing of magic sizzled behind my eyes.

"He says there's a piece of some sand clock that can control time trapped behind this door. We have to go through a maze, into a castle, and get it back."

"Where are the other pieces?" Apollo asked, his arms folded and the look on his face questioning the legitimacy of my words.

I wondered if he thought I was still making it up. I would have been flattered that he thought I had that vivid of an imagination if he did.

"I'm not sure, but right now our main concern is this one. That is, unless you want to be stuck in a time loop for a hundred years like he has." I said, shutting down the conversation.

Apollo huffed, but he didn't fight it anymore.

My eyes darted from each of their faces, waiting to hear any more hesitations, but they were all silent now, even Silas.

"Okay then, let's do this." I made my way to the golden door, and before I could even reach out to try to push it, it slid open.

The sound of rock grinding against rock cut through the stale air inside of the temple, and rays of light shot out in all directions, flooding into the open doorway.

I shielded my eyes, giving them a few seconds to adjust to the intense shift in light before I pulled my hand away and my mouth hung open.

In front of me was a cobblestone walkway, with hedges so high on either side that I'd have to climb to even get a chance at seeing over them.

"Well boys," I sighed, knowing there was no way I could turn back now. "Here we go."

Chapter Seventeen

I stepped through the threshold of the doorway and a cool rush of wind swept over me, leaving an icy layer of goosebumps in its wake.

The air felt lighter there, crisper like it was still the wee hours of the morning. I spun around to see who was going to follow after me, but to my surprise the door had disappeared and there was nothing but a thick green hedge that created a dead end behind me.

"What the hell?" I muttered, sticking my arm forward.

I'd thought that it could have been some sort of optical illusion and my hand would phase right through it, but it was as real as the nose on my face.

I pulled my hand from the rough leaves and groaned. I took a few steps forward, taking me down the cobblestone path when Apollo appeared out of nowhere, standing right in front of me.

"That was a little bit of a rush, wasn't it?" He shivered, getting the bout of coldness out of his system.

Behind him came Atlas then Adler.

I waited for Silas to emerge from the same spot that the others had, but instead he appeared behind me.

"Looking for me are we, love?" He whispered over my shoulder, and my skin erupted with goosebumps once again.

I jumped, and my heart raced with a small yelp escaping my lips. It was the cherry on top of the *this girl has definitely gone crazy* cake that I was serving to the other guys.

They all looked at me out of the corner of their eyes like I had completely lost my marbles.

"What?" I let my annoyance filter through my voice as I smoothed my shirt with my hand and straightened my posture.

I wasn't crazy.

I wasn't.

Hopefully getting through the maze and finding the sand clock would prove it to them.

Not like I had to in the first place.

A fire-wielding psycho burning shit to the ground— sure they'd believe it.

Three magical mages that had been asleep for a hundred years— sure they'd believe it.

A girl who had never had an ounce of magical ability in her life suddenly being able to control all four elements— yep, they'll believe it.

But a mage who is able to control time, being trapped in a realm where only I can see him sounds made up.

Makes sense.

"We should get moving." I said, ignoring all of their stares.

It was obvious which way we needed to go because there was a huge hedge blocking us from going backward, so I made the logical decision to start down the path.

I hadn't noticed how serene and quiet it was when we'd first came through, but the farther I made it down the long path, the more I realized that it was *too* quiet and serene.

"You said we're out in the garden, right?" I turned my head to Silas who walked beside me. "Why can't I hear any animals?"

I cocked my head to the side, stringing my ears for even the faintest chirp from a bird.

Nothing.

The mischief left his eyes, and a sadness lingered beneath the surface of the violet pools.

"Because, much like your world, mine has been frozen for quite some time now." He stared off ahead, but I could tell he was somewhere else. He had retreated somewhere deep inside his mind.

Somewhere painful.

"I was actually on a quest to find a way to break the curse, searching for the second half of the sand clock when I got trapped in a time loop too." His voice nearly cracked. and I saw a line of tears begin to form in his eyes. "That is, until you rescued me, madam." He recovered the pep in his step and blinked back the flood that threatened to spill.

And just like that, in a split second, he was back to his chipper, overly flamboyant self.

I wouldn't have been able to guess that he had even an ounce of trauma in his life by how cheerful and mischievous he always looked.

But it's crazy what kind of pain you can hide behind a smile.

I knew that all too well.

"Do you guys think we'll ever get used to her talking to herself like that?" Adler joked from behind, and the other guys chuckled.

I didn't bother spinning around, I just raised my arm, my middle finger high.

Sarcastic gasps came from behind.

"Innocent Eden wants us to fuck off?" Adler feigned surprise.

"Didn't you guys already do that to her today?" Apollo groaned.

"Didn't you already *try* to do that to me today?" I said back without missing a beat.

A wave of laughter erupted from Atlas and Adler, and a satisfactory smile spread across my lips.

It felt good to stick up for myself. I couldn't believe that I'd spent so many years missing out on the feeling.

I cringed when I thought about some of the things that I let people get away with doing to me, and I vowed that it would never happen again.

Not if I had anything to say about it.

It felt like we had been walking forever, but maybe that was just a side effect of being frozen in time.

Matter of fact, the entire day felt like it was dragging on.

I realized that I didn't know how long it had been since I'd slept.

Or eaten.

Or rested for that matter.

Up ahead the path finally halted, and we came to a fork in the road.

"When you said a maze in the garden, I didn't think you meant a maze that was as big as an entire freaking city!" I groaned. "I think we should stop for some rest."

"And some food." Adler added from behind.

I rolled my eyes at his constant hunger. It was like the man could only think about one thing at a time, and most of the time it was food.

I knew Apollo agreed, but he'd never admit it. He was the type of person who was so prideful he'd walk until he collapsed before admitting he was tired.

"If you guys need to rest that's okay." He shrugged before leaning his back up against the maze wall with his arms crossed.

"Good. I'm glad we got King Apollo's permission." I nodded in his direction. "But where are we supposed to get food? Do you want me to just pull it out of thin air? "

As fast as the words left my lips, Silas disappeared, leaving only a small wink of light behind. Even that faded quicker than I could comprehend.

And as fast as he had left, he returned, only this time it wasn't just him who appeared. He brought with him an entire dinner table, covered in steaming hot food.

It appeared in the middle of the walkway, and he disappeared a few more times, reappearing to drag back a chair for each of us to sit at.

The look on the guys' faces was priceless. The way the color drained from their cheeks alone made the hassle of the maze worth it.

After the initial shock passed, they all pounced at the meal, rushing to take a seat.

Even my stomach rumbled at the sight of the delicious food, which made me completely forget to grill him on how the heck he made all of it happen.

There were so many choices I didn't know where to start. There was a roasted turkey and a baked ham, even a decadent chicken sat in the middle. They were all surrounded by plates and plates of fruit, and vegetables.

I couldn't remember the last time I'd eaten a meal that smelled as mouthwatering at that one, let alone as magical.

"It literally looks like a feast fit for a king." I turned my sights to Silas.

"That's because it was, love."

My heart felt like it fell into my panties at the word. There was something about it paired with his accent that made it a panty melter.

"Hundred-year-old food. Yum." I joked.

Each of the guys froze, Adler with half a bite of a chicken leg hanging out of his mouth. Their eyes were all glued to me, horror written across their faces.

"Tell them it's fine, it's been frozen in time. It's as if it was just taken out of the oven."

Part of me wanted to watch them squirm a bit longer before I let them off the hook, but that would have required a whole lot of energy that I didn't have.

"He said it's fine. The time spell kept it fresh."

Under normal circumstances I had a feeling that they would have protested more. Thrown a fit or something, but we were all unusually ravenous, so my half-assed explanation was enough to send them diving back into its goodness.

Even I tore into a chicken leg with my teeth.

Silas sat in the seat beside me, watching with wonder in his eyes.

Again, under normal circumstances it would have felt even slightly awkward having an invisible stranger with bright purple hair practically hold me under a microscope while I ate, but circumstances were special.

"Take a picture, it'll last longer." I mumbled before casually tossing a grape into my mouth, savoring the sweet juices that erupted from it.

"Oh, trust me, I would gladly stare at your face for eternity if given the chance."

His words made me feel fuzzy inside.

I wondered if it was the accent that did it this time or was there really just something inside of me that needed to be shown love?

I felt different now, there was no doubt. The fire magic had made me rough around the edges. But deep down inside there was still a raw part of me showing, something that not even my fire magic could scald into submission.

That was the last nagging part of the old Eden, fighting tooth and nail to hold her ground.

If only she'd done that with everyone else, maybe the magic wouldn't have felt like I was something weak that needed scolding in the first place.

So many past regrets.

So many things that I couldn't wait to change once I got my hands on that sand clock thing.

"Wait a minute. If you were able to teleport inside, or whatever, and grab an entire table, chairs, and freaking feast why can't you just teleport into the castle and grab the sand clock. You do that and boom, our problems are all solved." I said the words so confident that I'd found the easy way to get to the bottom of our issues. "And then while you're at it you can teleport us back to the manor."

"You look so lovely when you think you've got it figured out." Silas leaned his face against his fist, his arm propped up on the table. "If I was able to do so, don't you think I would have already done it by now?"

"I don't know, I thought maybe you liked watching me squirm to figure things out." I shrugged and tossed another grape in my mouth.

"I do love to see a little mouse work its way through a maze to get some cheese. Unfortunately, I can't touch the sand clock, nobody can but you."

I blinked at his words, my mind slowly hanging on to each one.

"What? Why am I the only one who can touch the clock?"

"Because you're an eden, right? It was made by the edens as a weapon, only to be used if absolutely necessary. So, as you can imagine, it was created with a few counter-protection measures."

"Like what?"

"Oh, nothing big really. Just being trapped in a time loop for a hundred years or so." Silas said the words so casually and pretended to shift his gaze elsewhere.

I raised a brow, my mind finally catching up. I would have sworn my mind was the one trapped in a loop of frozen time.

"Are you saying that's how you got stuck there?"

"I will neither confirm nor deny it." He held his right hand up like he was about to swear himself in on a holy book.

I opened my mouth to protest but was cut off by the abrupt rumble that came from the ground beneath our feet. It sounded like the ground was cracking somewhere deep inside the earth.

"What is that?" I turned to Silas, with my eyes full of panic.

"It looks like the guardians have awakened."

Chapter Eighteen

"Guardians? What guardians? You didn't mention any guardians!" I barked at Silas angrily.

"Yikes. You're an angry little mouse now, aren't you?" Silas said before taking a single fingertip and booping it against the tip of my nose.

The rumble beneath us continued now, only louder this time.

A fiery anger rose up inside of me at how casually Silas was handling it all.

I clenched my fists tightly, trying to hold in the anger that threatened to blow the lid off of me like I was a mason jar full of it, waiting to spill it everywhere.

"Eden, what is your imaginary friend saying?" Adler's voice was uneasy, but it only made me angrier.

"I don't like being lied to." I stood up letting my chair topple over behind me and hovered over Silas, fists still clenched tightly.

"Hey, let's settle down." Silas held up two hands. "I didn't lie, I just didn't tell you the whole truth."

I couldn't control myself anymore. My fists burst into two balls of flames and I hurled them at Silas.

He quickly phased out of the chair, and with a wink of light appeared on the other side of the table.

"Hey! I said I'm sorry!" He quickly ducked down to dodge a bunch of grapes that I chucked at his head.

"No, you didn't!" I ripped a warm leg off of the roasted turkey and flung that too.

"Well I meant to!" Silas teleported to the right, nearly too late and his death certificate almost read *death by turkey leg.*

"Almost doesn't count!" I resorted to picking up the entire turkey, my hands bursting it into flames, its dry skin charring easily.

Silas' eyes widened, but a smirk fell on his lips.

Like I said— mischievous.

I flung the entire flaming turkey in his direction and he dodged it just in time for it to hit the ground, splattering flaming molten fragments in all directions.

All three of the guys still sat planted at the table, a look of horror in their eyes.

And right there, with impending doom closing in on us quick, and the mysterious rumble in my ears I busted out laughing.

It was the one of the deepest, hardest, most infectious belly laughs that I'd ever felt, just like with Adler. Whoever had too many laughs like that?

My stomach muscles ached, and the more the guys' eyes widened, the more the louder my laugh got.

I couldn't help but imagine what I must have looked like, throwing flaming food at nothing. I couldn't even begin to comprehend what I must have looked like screaming at thin air.

But it was the looks on their faces that got me. The look in their eyes that frosted the cake for me.

I looked up at Silas through the blur of tears in my eyes and he cracked up too, a hearty laugh escaping his lips. It was hard to hear over the rumbling of the earth beneath us, but it was there.

A steady stream of tears ran from my eyes down my cheeks, and I thought I was going to pee my pants.

It was all fun and games until there was a loud boom from far down the walkway that we had come from, and the rumbling stopped.

My laugh was cut off immediately and the smile slowly faded from my face.

The guys' attention snapped from me to the walkway.

In the not-so-far distance I noticed a large figure, almost as tall as the hedges, moving toward us— fast.

It took longer than I'd care to admit to register what was happening inside my brain.

"Guys," The word fell from my lips. "Run."

Without asking a single question the guys shoved the table over, toppling all the precious food onto the dirty ground.

If my life wasn't in danger I would have been pretty upset at the sight, but I did just light an entire turkey on fire so that didn't leave me much room to complain about the waste of such a delicious meal.

Without missing a single beat, they pushed the table on its side and positioned it to serve as a small barricade.

It wasn't much, definitely to a giant like that, but it was all we had in the form of defense at the moment.

I wildly shifted my gaze from one side of the forked pathway to another.

"Which way do we go?" I asked, panic in my voice.

"You're supposed to know! This was all on you!" Apollo's familiar anger returned.

I wanted to turn around and smack him once. Or fuck him so he'd finally stop whining about it. I would have traded my left tit if it meant I didn't have to deal with his attitude anymore.

The giant's thunderous steps were approaching, clouding my thoughts.

I closed my eyes and called on the power of wind, hoping that my firepower hadn't clouded my ability to use the other elements.

Beneath me a whirlwind formed, creating a gust powerful enough to lift me from the ground.

I rose higher and higher, nearing the top of the hedge.

Fly up, see which way to go, and take it— that was the plan.

Easy right?

Wrong.

The second I neared the top of the hedge I smashed my head on an invisible barrier, a wave of pain flowing through my eye and resting at the back of my skull.

The pain threw me off of my concentration and I spiraled toward the ground even faster than I had risen.

Too fast for the guys to move— except Silas.

In a wink of light, Silas appeared underneath me, catching me in his arms.

I looked up at him with one hand on my head.

Up close I could see the dark purple specks of color that littered his violet eyes, and the tiny freckles that dotted his nose.

Meanwhile the guys all stared in disbelief at me floating seamlessly above the ground.

"Who's imaginary now?" I turned to Adler with a smirk on my face.

Before he had a chance to reply a thunderous roar cut through the air, and Silas dropped me to the ground.

I landed rough, scratching up my back against the cobblestone.

I looked up at Silas angrily and he held both hands up again.

"Sorry, that was a bit of an accident."

There went any magical moment that we might have been having.

I turned to look back down the walkway. The beast was frighteningly close now. Close enough for me to make out what the hell it was— a rock giant.

It was made up completely of boulders and stones, all a shade of dull gray that matched the stone of the walkway.

It was angry, and sharp, jagged rocks stuck out of its mouth.

Even if it weren't a giant, I wouldn't want to have to square off with it. A rock fist to the face didn't sound very enjoyable to me.

I jumped to my feet, a wave of adrenaline dulling the pain that I felt in my backside. I knew the pain would catch up to me eventually, but I had to be alive for it to do that, so I had hoped.

I held my hands out in front of me and welcomed the earth magic to flow through me like a conduit. I focused all of my concentration on the hedges, willing my energy to flow from my hands and into them.

It took a few seconds, but slowly the hedge in front of us started to grow out and into the walkway until a fully formed hedge was placed in between the beast and us like a dead end.

"That's not going to hold a beast like that for long. We need to go— now!"

I commanded.

I had absolutely no idea which path was the right one, not the slightest clue. What I did know was that if we sat around long enough to deliberate and make an informed decision, we were toasted. So I grabbed Apollo's hand and dragged him down the passage to the right.

I grabbed him because I knew he would be the one to give me the most grief and question why I chose the path I did.

Both things that we didn't have time for.

As quickly as I could I set off, nearly ripping his shoulder out of the socket.

He seemed to soften at the feel of my hand in his, the contact melting the hard exterior that he tried so hard to hold on to.

But again— it was the wrong time.

Now was the perfect time that we needed his anger. It seemed like elemental magic was highly influenced by emotions, which was probably one of the reasons why Apollo was so powerful to begin with.

We rounded the corner and I breathed a sigh of relief when I didn't smack into an immediate dead end. It was a good sign, and we needed some of those right about then.

The others followed us closely, just as I'd expected and for a second I was hopeful about my hedge barrier. It was holding up surprisingly well against the guardian.

But as always right when I got my hopes up, they came clattering down once again.

There was a loud noise like twigs snapping, and I knew that the beast had made its way through the hedge. The thunderous steps resumed behind us once again before pausing.

He's at the fork.

Internally I screamed to the universe to cut me a break this one time and have the beast choose the wrong pathway, but the universe is merciless, and the thundering resumed behind us. I could tell by the intensity of the vibrations.

We took a sharp right and were caught at a fork once again. I didn't even hesitate this time, cutting a sharp right. The guys followed closely behind and we started to get some distance between the thundering steps and us. Things were looking up.

That wasn't until we rounded a corner and were met with a dead end.

Fuck.

"Fuck!" I screamed into the sky impulsively cursing the universe.

It wasn't smart, I knew it the second that the word left my lips and cut into the otherwise quiet air.

The thundering steps stopped as the monster reached the fork and listened for the location of my scream.

There were three pairs of angry eyes staring back at me, something that would have completely obliterated the old Eden.

In the past I could never have dealt with people being angry at me, it was my number one fear. But now, after all of this work, and all the magic coursing through me, I quite simply didn't give a shit what they thought of me.

It was a stupid decision, and I recognized that the second the air left my lungs, but it was a decision that was already made.

Without the sand clock I had no way of going back and fixing it, so I was left to deal with the consequences like a big girl.

The thundering steps resumed, and I let go of Apollo's hand, letting it drop lazily at his side.

I shoved my way past the other guys and Silas appeared in the corner of the walkway. Even his eyes were wide with anticipation of what was to come.

They all knew the kind of power that lay inside of me, but they doubted me. I could feel it.

I didn't blame them because up until a few days ago I doubted myself too. I didn't think that I deserved the magic that I had, and I definitely didn't think I could control it.

If you had told me a month before that I was about to take on a mystical rock monster by myself, willingly, I wouldn't have believed it. Not for a single second.

But there I was, feet-planted and hands raised.

For a split second it felt like time slowed, and my past flashed before my eyes.

Every time someone had told me I couldn't do something, every time I was mistreated was shown in my mind.

I didn't want to be that person anymore, the kind that believed those things.

Beneath the surface of my skin magic sizzled. It wasn't just fire magic though. It was all four. I could feel the different types mixing together for a blend of magic that I'd never experienced before.

The monster rounded the corner, going so fast that it nearly lost its footing. As it ran it used its long rock claws to dig into the walkway and propel itself further.

I took a deep breath and my heart didn't skip a single beat.

It was my time, and I knew it.

I closed my eyes and let the magic flow through me, before

opening them again, my eyes glowing a bright shade of blue.

All four types of magic flowed through me at once, ripping through my skin exposing a pain that I had never felt before. I screamed, revealing a beam of blue light from my mouth, my eyes and both of my hands. The light connected with the rock creature and it exploded, shards of rock and dust flying everywhere before a huge surge of magic exploded from me and was sent out in all directions with a deafening boom.

My body was met with the harsh cobblestone and my vision went black.

Chapter Nineteen

My hearing came back to me first in the form of the worst ringing in my ears that I'd ever experienced. It sounded over and over again until my jaw ached. Next came my sense of touch, as I felt the harsh stone beneath me, and every muscle in my body screaming out for help. Last came my vision, with the blackness slowly retreating and my eyes learning to focus all over again. I lay flat on my back and my lungs erupted in a fit of coughing at the debris that littered the air and smoke that was clearing.

My eyes focused on Silas hovering over me, looking me in the face.

"Are you okay love? Bloody hell that was crazy!" His lips couldn't help but curl when he said the words. He was impressed by my power; it was written all over his face.

I sat up, wincing at the piercing pain that streaked through my side. Adler, Atlas and Apollo were all collecting themselves from the ground, their faces littered with soot and dirt.

Their eyes once again wide, but this time with admiration.

My jaw hung open at the sight of what was around me, the entire maze was gone. Completely obliterated. All that was left were the cobblestone pathways and empty spaces in between that snaked around in odd angles where the hedges once stood.

"Centuries." Silas offered a hand and pulled me from my seat. "That's how long the enchanted maze stood, guarding our realm from intruders. It was spelled by the strongest mages in history and it held up for centuries, designed to hold back any force— except you."

I didn't know if the tone in his voice was impressed or angry, so I shrugged.

"Sorry, I guess." My voice was hoarse.

I tried to take a step forward, but my muscles gave way beneath my weight and my leg wobbled. Down I spiraled toward the pavement again when a small tornado of wind appeared under me, and Atlas ran to my side.

He scooped me up, throwing my arm around his shoulder, and Apollo was quickly at the other side. They both held me up, but I was so exhausted that my chin clung to my chest.

A force of magic that powerful was insane. I wouldn't have believed it came from me if it didn't feel like my soul had been completely sucked from my body.

"You've depleted your magic source, darling. You need a top-up." Silas' voice sounded farther away as I weaved in and out of consciousness. "Tell them to take you into the castle. There's an infirmary there, first room on your right."

"Take me… to the… castle." I struggled to get the words out. I gathered enough strength to raise my chin from my chest, my eyes falling on the glorious castle that stood just outside of the confines of the maze.

The stone was a dark shade of grey, that could have almost been considered black if you looked at it in the right sunlight. Four gothic towers stretched into the sky, framing it on all corners.

All the windows held black shutters that were closed tightly.

"Infirmary… to the right."

Those were all the words my body would let me get out.

Silas was right, whatever fueled the magic inside of me had been completely obliterated. I felt like the rock beast, like I'd shatter into a billion different pieces at any second, crushed to a fine powder.

Apollo and Atlas drug me forward, my feet dragging behind us. I didn't even have the energy to pick them up. Adler led the pack as they tried to navigate what was left of the walkways to avoid having to drag me through the rough patches of exposed earth where the hedges had once been.

I felt myself slipping away. Whether it was into a deep slumber or the warm embrace of death, I couldn't tell you.

But I was in so much pain that I was at the point where I wouldn't have minded either.

After they'd hit the third dead end, I heard Apollo mumble *screw it.* Before telling Atlas to use his wind power to take us there.

"I don't know if that's a good idea. The wind force makes it pretty hard to breathe traveling like that, even for a short distance of time. She's hardly breathing as it is." Atlas argued, but Apollo wasn't having it.

"Just do it!" He growled. "Or she won't be breathing at all in a few minutes. I'm not losing her."

His words stopped abruptly like he hadn't meant for them to slip out with the rest, but they did and now he couldn't take them back.

Atlas groaned, weighing his options for only a second before sighing.

The wind around us picked up and after a few seconds I felt my feet get swept from underneath me.

Atlas was right. The wind whipping wouldn't have been a problem normally, but having barely enough strength to keep my eyes open, let alone force my lungs to work any harder, made my chest seize up.

I couldn't muster the energy to make my lungs fight against the wind blowing directly in my face, and my chest heaved involuntarily, sending immense waves of pain rippling through my rib cage.

I writhed, nearly slipping from their grip, the involuntary movement sapping whatever energy I might have had left.

"She can't breathe man!" Atlas's voice cracked. I could tell he was either crying, or close to tears and it broke my heart. "I have to stop man, I have to."

I felt the wind slowly dissipate until Apollo spoke up.

"No! We're almost there. Keep going or I swear to gods." The amount of gruff anger in his voice was new, even for him and my heart broke for Atlas even more. He wore his heart on his sleeve.

The edges of my consciousness blurred, and I felt my eyes roll back in my head. Right before I was welcomed into the darkness my feet touched down on the rough cobblestone path and the wind died down enough for me to take in a breath of air.

There was a pause, a single moment where everyone was completely still, until my lungs took in a big inhale, stretching the already sore muscles in my chest.

"Thank gods." Atlas exhaled.

I opened my eyes just a sliver and saw the entry stairs that led up to a grand wooden door with intricate golden molding spread across it in swirls. Adler kicked the doors open with his foot, quite dramatically I might add, before even testing it with his hands.

The old wooden door creaked open, revealing an even grander entryway, illuminated by a luxurious-looking candlelit chandelier.

The flames were still lit. It was odd to see them give off light, but not flicker and sway.

Apollo and Atlas helped me through the doorway and immediately cut to the right, entering the first room they saw.

Silas was right, there was an infirmary.

I felt them lay me on the small bed. I didn't know if it was just because I was in such rough shape or not, but the bed felt marvelously soft.

All I wanted to do was close my eyes and drift off.

I let the sliver close, engulfing me back in the welcoming darkness when I felt Silas' hot breath on the side of my face.

"Don't you dare try to fall asleep, love, I've just gotten started with you." There was a hint of joking in his voice, but I could tell that his worry was real.

Me closing my eyes and not having the strength to open them back up again was a real possibility.

I heard glass bottles clinking together as the guys rummaged through a cabinet nearby, searching for something that would help.

"How are we supposed to know what the hell is in these bottles?" The panic in Apollo's voice was slowly rising.

"Tell Apollo to grab the blue one by his left hand." Silas whispered in my ear.

"Blue... by your... left hand." I managed to spit the words out, each one siphoning more energy from me.

I felt like a car running on E, slowly sputtering as the last bit of gas in the tank is used up.

I could only coast on for so long.

I heard Apollo rush across the room and felt his hand gently slide underneath my head. He helped me raise my head just a little before bringing the mouth of a bottle to my lips.

I couldn't help but notice that it was the most gentle he'd ever

170

been with me.

I liked that side of him.

It was too bad it took me being on my literal deathbed to bring it out.

I remembered what Adler had said about the girl he loved, and how the fire magic had killed her.

Was that what he thought was going to happen to me?

I hated Apollo, but I loved him at the same time. It was one of those contradictions that doesn't make any sense at all but works at the same time.

Every fiber of Apollo's being found a way to get underneath my skin, especially now that my fire magic had gone awry, but every fiber found a way to stroke my soul while it was there.

And all I knew was that I wouldn't trade that feeling for the world.

The liquid was bubbly like soda as it touched my lips, and it smelled sweet like blueberries.

Unfortunately, it didn't taste like that either.

It tasted like a hybrid of wet dog and old sock and left a feeling on my tongue like it was made of fur.

My stomach wretched at the taste and I spit a little back out.

Apollo pulled the bottle from my lips and gave me a second to recover. He must have set it down on the bed beside me because he still had one hand underneath my head and used the other one to move a piece of hair from my face.

I felt him gently stroke the side of my cheek with the back of his finger and whisper to me.

"You have to drink it all, okay? I know it probably tastes like shit, but dying is worse, let me tell you."

The side of my mouth twitched, my half-assed attempt at a smile but he knew what I was doing.

"Tall, dark and angry is right, I'm afraid." Silas' voice came from farther across the room.

I slowly nodded my head.

As tired as I was, as much pain that I was in, I couldn't bring myself to be selfish. The selfish thing to do would have been to close my eyes and let myself slip into oblivion. It would have saved the world from my fire magic, it would have ended my eternal battle with my own mind, but it would have doomed all four of them to an eternity stuck in a magical loop.

And it would have damned Apollo to reliving the most traumatic thing he'd ever gone through.

I couldn't be that person— old Eden, or new— it wasn't me.

I felt the bottle press back against my lips and I held my breath, letting the bubbling liquid fill my mouth.

I suppressed my gag and drank in big gulps, letting the liquid simmer its way down my throat until the bottle was completely turned upside down.

Empty.

Meanwhile my stomach was full of the sizzling concoction. It created a bubbling feeling in my abdomen that slowly radiated out, spreading to my chest and my legs until I felt like a beehive filled with busy worker bees.

Every inch of my skin tingled and buzzed, but Silas was right, I felt my strength coming back. It started off slowly at first, but gradually snowballed until I was able to wiggle a finger, then a toe, and then all at once.

I even wiggle my nose, for no reason other than I could.

I slowly opened my eyes and waited for them to adjust to the dim light inside the infirmary.

Potion or not, they were still heavy to hold open.

I looked up to see Apollo sitting at my bedside, and if I didn't know any better I would have sworn I saw the dried stains where tears spewed from his eyes, but I convinced myself that must have just been a trick of the lighting.

A bright smile spread across his face— a genuine one.

It wasn't a smirk or a mischievous grin. It was a smile, and even a blind man would have been able to tell that it came from a place of genuine happiness.

Our differences aside I had to admit that maybe Apollo had sides to him that he didn't let other people see. Maybe he was more than a sexy sack of testosterone potatoes with water magic. Maybe he was just waiting for life to give him a reason to be able to open himself up again.

And maybe life was giving me a reason to let him.

I opened my mouth to say something, but he brought a finger to my lips.

"Sleep. You need it. I need it. We all need it." He spoke the truth.

"There are enough beds in this place to choke a horse, and we have nothing but time."

He half laughed at his own joke.

I wanted to protest. Part of me wanted to do nothing but finish our task. I wanted out of this time loop and I wanted to skip to the part where I mastered the element. There were things I had to clean up, and I got a devilish new idea on something to change.

But a different part of me knew he was right.

I let my eyelids close like heavy metal doors, slamming shut.

And before I knew it, the darkness that I'd craved welcomed me back.

Chapter Twenty

I didn't know how long I was out when I finally clawed my way to the surface of my consciousness.

It was impossible to tell. The sun in the sky didn't budge, and if there were any clocks in the castle I knew they'd be frozen.

It had to be quite some time, though, because I felt more rested than I'd ever been.

My eyes crept open, and I found myself staring up at the dark stone ceiling.

The room was as quiet as I remembered the maze in the garden to be.

Across the small room, I saw Adler and Atlas sitting on the floor with their backs leaned up against the wall. Their eyes were closed and Adler let out a faint snore that made me want to laugh. They both rested their heads against each other. I didn't know if it was intentional or not, but it was cute all the same.

Beside me Apollo sat in a chair with his head slumped to his chest. It rose and fell every now and then with movements, but he was out cold too.

Must have been all that turkey that we ate. I thought. *Or the running for our lives. Either one, it's impossible to know.*

I pulled myself up to sit and noticed the bed beneath me was soaked.

What the–

"Yeah, you looked like you were having quite steamy dreams." Silas said, his voice slicing through the silence and making me jump.

I almost shushed him, before I realized I was the only one who could hear him anyway.

I held my fingertip up against my lips and gestured silently toward the others.

Silas nodded and I slowly got off the bed, sure not to make a single noise otherwise Apollo would be up in a snap of my fingers.

I slid off the comforters and brushed off my clothes before I noticed how they were singed at the edges.

I looked up at Silas with confusion in my eyes and he just shrugged.

"Like I said before, your dreams must have been pretty hot."

I turned to see the bed I was lying on nearly charred, the only untouched place was in the shape of my body in the center of the bed.

Even in my sleep I almost burned the place down.

I fought the urge to groan and quietly slipped out of the room, closing the door behind me.

Silas appeared next to me and started to say something, but I held my finger to my lips again and slowly crept down the cold stone hallway.

I waited until we were far enough away to speak.

"Where is this sand clock thing?" I said.

"Well, you're straight to business when you wake up in the morning, aren't you?" Silas raised a brow.

"I have things I have to do."

"What? When time's frozen?"

"No, after."

Silas thought for a moment, connecting the dots.

"You want to clean up your timeline." He said it like a lightbulb had gone off in his head.

I kept my eyes laser straight and tried to play stupid. "I have no idea what that means."

It wasn't necessarily a lie.

"That may be true, but it's what you're trying to do. You're trying to clean up your timelines. Erase your mistakes. Fix your wrongs. Am I getting it right?"

I kept my focus on the hallway forward.

"If you won't help me find it, I'll just find it myself."

I picked up my pace, like that was going to do something. The man could teleport at will. There wasn't anywhere I could hide, but it made me feel good and rebellious.

Two things the old Eden wouldn't have dared find solace in.

"Hey, hey, hey, I never said I wouldn't help. My father? That man would have said no, believe me. But I have to warn you, that's dangerous stuff. One wrong move, and your entire life is different. You might think it's something small, like killing an ant on the sidewalk, but in the scheme of time and space it becomes bigger and bigger until you come back to your place in the timeline and the entire world has ended."

His words were enough to make my feet clamp together. I stopped in the middle of the hallway taking them all in.

I'd never thought of that.

He looked at me, watching my thoughts whizz past my eyes at a million miles a second.

"I never said not to do it though."

I looked up at him, finally connecting the dots.

"That's how you ended up imprisoned, isn't it?" I raised a brow, going off nothing but a hunch.

His violet eyes shifted from mine, uncomfortable beneath my gaze.

"No one said all of that." He half laughed.

"You didn't have to." I put a hand on my hip. "Now spill it. What were you trying to do? You had to have been trying to fix something in the timeline."

"I was trying to kill a fire mage, to prevent the end of the world as we know it."

I blinked a few times, trying to comprehend what he was saying.

It was Asher, it had to have been because they were all encased around the same time.

I knew it was the same thing I was trying to do, but something inside of me hurt at his words, and that itself made me feel gross.

Was I condoning all the hate that Asher spewed?

He'd tried to kill me more times than I could count on one hand.

It was his fault, after all, that my fire magic had been activated.

But why did I suddenly feel sick at the thought of him dying?

"Fucking spark." I mumbled beneath my breath and spun on one heel to continue down the hallway.

"I'm sorry?" Silas called from behind me, still trying to figure out what the hell just happened.

I didn't have time to explain. I needed to get my hands on that sand clock and fast. I wasn't going to let a change of heart keep me from having the world, and I definitely wasn't going to let it keep me from getting my piping hot revenge.

With a wink of light Silas appeared ahead of me blocking my path.

"Can you stop and listen to me for one moment, please?" His accent almost got thicker when he was frustrated.

"Absolutely not." I shoved past him.

"Can you not let anyone help you? Are you that daft that you can't recognize a friend standing right in front of you trying to help you for your own good?"

His words stung and made me stop in my tracks with my back turned to him.

An ache grew in my heart the size of Texas.

Friend? I didn't know what that word meant anymore.

My entire life I'd only ever had one— Jade.

I threw everything I'd had into her. I built my life around the companionship she gave me, and she threw me away the first chance she got.

When it came to friends, I was more than scarred, I was scorched, and the burn still ached every second of every day.

"I don't have friends." I said coldly before continuing down the hallway and turning to the right.

From behind me I heard Silas groan loudly.

If I was good at doing one thing now, it was pushing people away.

I'd spent my entire life hoping someone would notice me, praying for love, and now I had four guys practically begging to have the opportunity to do that and I just *couldn't.*

I'd never felt more broken than that moment.

I wished time wasn't frozen so I could track down my mother. I was pretty sure this kind of thing was in a mother's expertise, but I wasn't sure because I'd never had one of those either.

I guess I just wanted to have someone who had to love me no matter what. No matter how hard I pushed, no matter how scalding hot my temper got. I wanted someone who didn't have the choice whether to stay or go.

Someone who chose me for me and that was that.

That included pushover me, crybaby me, socially awkward me, and yes— even hothead me.

I needed someone who was in for it all, but at the same time I felt bad for putting people through those things.

Long story short, I didn't make any fucking sense.

And I also had no idea where I was going.

I stopped walking and waited.

Three. Two. One.

Almost right on cue Silas appeared through a blink of light and stood in front of me.

He opened his mouth, his lungs equipped with a full stock of breath, ready to start a long- winded response. He'd probably been thinking about it the whole time. Preparing it, but I stopped it before it had even started.

"Okay." I said, with a slight smile on my face. I probably looked awkward now when I actually tried to look friendly.

"Okay?" Silas' once pointed finger drooped at the knuckle illustrating his confusion.

"Okay. I need help." I said. "From a friend."

The word made Silas smile, and I smiled inside too.

I realized I needed to stop pushing people away just to test the limits of their love. I needed to stop putting my relationships through the wringer just to see if they'd survive. I needed to be comfortable and confident enough in what I brought to the table that I didn't live in fear that they'd go eat with someone less complicated.

Those were all parts of the old Eden. Residue that she'd left behind.

I didn't want to be the old Eden anymore. I didn't want to be pushover Eden, or crybaby Eden, or even angry, fire-wielding Eden.

I wanted to stop letting my emotions control how I responded. I wanted to stop letting my *magic* control how I responded.

From then on out, I was in control.

Plain old Eden.

And that was enough for me.

I followed Silas down the hall, and he led me into a small dimly lit room with no windows.

In the front of the room sat a shimmering golden chest, just like the one in the temple.

I was mesmerized by the sparkling flecks that it held beneath its surface.

"I recognize this." I said. "There was one like it in the temple back home. When it opened, a beast flew out and exploded. That was what froze the entire world." I turned to look at him, and our eyes met. "And what led me to you."

Silas' eyes widened. "You mean you've opened one before? All I did was touch the bloody thing and I was banished to a century stuck between worlds!" He huffed, and I couldn't help but giggle.

"How did you open it?" He asked.

His gaze fell heavy on my skin, as he waited for the secret to cracking the chest.

My mind traveled back to my time in the temple with Atlas. The things that had to happen for me to let out a surge of magic that was just right to match the frequency of the chest.

"Oh, with magic. Nothing big really."

"Well then, do it again." Silas said eagerly.

My cheeks grew a warm shade of red. He didn't know what he was saying, of course, but it still sent shivers between my legs.

"I can't." I said, a sudden wave of nerves flowing through me.

"And why's that?" Silas asked curiously as he closed in the space between us.

I weighed my options. I thought about lying or saying that I didn't think I had enough strength, but that would be stupid.

I didn't want to start our— whatever this was— out with petty lies.

He was standing so close now that I could feel his breath brushing against my body.

"Because, it only happens when I climax."

Silas raised a brow and the mischievous grin of his returned, making my skin erupt in goosebumps.

"Well then, darling, we'll just have to make you climax then. Won't we?"

Before I could fully process what he said, he pulled me in for a kiss and I kissed him back.

Chapter Twenty-One

Silas's lips were the softest that I'd ever felt, and everything about him was different from the others, all the way down to the way that he held my head when he kissed me.

His passion was a mix of sweet and playful, two things that I gladly welcomed.

There was an electric magic feeling that sparked between our lips as they brushed against each other, and I let myself get lost in the moment.

I let myself surrender all the things inside my head that I'd let torture me. I surrendered all of my inhibitions, everything, and I let myself work on my lust alone.

I had to admit to myself that I'd been thinking about the way his hands would feel caressing my bare skin the entire time. Since the moment I saw him I tried to lie to myself about it, even after we'd sparked. But it was no use.

The universe wanted us together, just like it wanted me with the others.

And what the universe wanted, it got.

What was the point in fighting it?

I slipped my tongue into Silas' mouth, flicking the tip of his playfully as I slid my hands underneath the collar of his jumpsuit.

I didn't know who dressed him the morning he was banished, or what, but it was not a sex friendly outfit.

He gladly let the fabric fall from his shoulders and into a crumpled heap on the floor. He was skinny, that was for sure, but that was because most of his body was made up of chiseled muscle. From his chest, to his abs, even down to his legs he was definitely the kind of person who worked out.

I let my fingertips glide from his collarbone, over his rippled chest, across the ridges of his abs, and down to the elastic of his boxers. I shimmied my fingers underneath and released his stiff cock from them too as they slid down his legs and joined his other clothes in a pile on the floor.

My mouth watered at the sight of him hard, waiting for me.

Before I could even dream about stuffing it into my mouth, Silas pulled my shirt up and flung it across the room. The room was a lot colder than I'd expected it to be, and my stomach broke out in goosebumps. My nipples grew stiff even though they were still shielded by the fabric of my bra.

It was a stone castle, so it made sense that I was freezing my nipples off. I guess I'd just always imagined castles a lot warmer when I saw them in storybooks and television.

Silas' lips migrated from my mouth, to my jawline, down my neck, and finally landed on my collarbone before he unbuttoned my jeans and I wiggled out of them.

The anticipation alone was sending my pussy into overdrive. I almost could have come just by the thick sexual tension that clung to the air between us.

I stood in front of Silas with nothing but my bra and panties. He paused for a moment, seemingly devouring me with those gorgeous purple eyes of his.

"What?" I asked and my cheeks burned beneath his gaze.

"I'm just admiring the beauty of your body love." His voice was gruff and primal.

The closer we got to sex it was like the further he strayed from his sweet playful self, and gravitated toward an instinctual, passionate arousal.

Something that I had not seen coming but also welcomed.

It was like his soft, mischievous edges got sharper the harder his cock got, and the more time went on, the more I did feel like a little mouse caught in the sights of a ravenous cat.

And judging by how stiff he was, he was ready to pounce at any second.

He reached around behind me and unclipped my bra, chucking that across the room too. My breasts bounced slightly as they were released from their prison before resuming their normal, perky position.

He dropped my panties and I stepped out of them. I didn't wait for him to make the first move, where's the fun in that?

I dropped to my knees, wincing at the harsh stone floor that I'd forgotten, but it was too late to turn back.

His cock was long, which matched his height. I wrapped my fingers around it and looked up at him innocently as I started to stroke him slowly.

His dick pulsated in my hand as he got harder and harder, looking down at me.

I stuck my tongue out and held eye contact as ever so slowly I ran the tip of it up the length of his shaft. I took my time, enjoying every inch of his glorious member.

Watching him squirm wasn't too bad either.

I reached the tip and spun a few circles around it before taking it all the way in my mouth.

I let it slide all the way into my throat, sure to squeeze it tightly.

"Oh my little mouse, you are exquisite." He moaned beneath his breath.

I pulled his dick from my throat just as slowly as it had entered and came up for air. My eyes watered and the tears rushed down my cheeks, but I had a feeling the sight only turned Silas on more before he took the liberty of thrusting back into my throat this time.

His dick was so long that I didn't have a choice but to deep throat it. There was no other way that it would make it all the way into my mouth.

I didn't have much experience with someone throat-fucking me, but Silas slowly picked up speed and it gave my body enough time to adjust.

Before I knew it, his dick was gliding in and out of my throat at a speed that was almost hard for me to register, and his hand was tangled in the back of my hair.

There was a wink of light and suddenly my mouth was empty. I probably looked pretty stupid going in for another throat fuck when nothing was there.

Just when I realized what was going on, Silas appeared behind me and pushed me down on all fours.

"Your body is perfection." He moaned.

I felt the head of his dick positioned perfectly to enter me from behind. I couldn't tell if his dick was dripping wet, or if it was my pussy, but either way he had no problems prying me open and shoving his cock inside.

I felt every inch of him fill me, and I had no doubts that there was still a lot to spare that he wasn't able to stuff inside of me because he'd already reached my limit.

He didn't waste any time, and he didn't bother starting off gentle. I could tell that we were both at the same place, our sexual instincts were guiding us now. Something as old as time itself guiding us, and we weren't going to stop until we both climaxed.

He fucked me from behind, his dick pressing a spot deep inside me that I'd never had touched before. I didn't know what it was, all I knew was that it sent waves of pleasure washing through my body in ways that I couldn't have ever imagined.

The low simmer of magic started to build up inside my pelvis, threatening to spill over in a blast any second.

He massaged my insides before fucking me so hard that I thought he would rearrange them.

Soft moans escaped my lips before they erupted into loud screams as he thrust in ways that were hard for me to even fathom.

My body seized up, my pussy clamping down on his cock hard enough to throw him into a climax. My body shook, the feel of his warm liquid only making me cum harder, and there was an eruption of light blue magic that I recognized as all the elements at once.

It pulsated out from me, and just like before the chest absorbed every last drop of it before opening.

Silas pulled his cock from me and I felt the surge of his cum filling the space where his dick once was.

There was no better feeling than being filled with someone's cum, there was no convincing me otherwise.

I took a second to catch my breath, a sex smile permanently stuck to my face.

Silas beamed too, looking at me slyly out of the corner of his eye to see if I was watching.

After I'd finally gotten enough oxygen replenished in my lungs, I scrambled to get my clothes on, the reality of actually opening the chest slowly hitting me.

I slid my legs into my panties and pulled my pants on, wondering what the sand clock would look like. Was it how I'd imagined it?

Would it hurt to touch?

Was there any way I could just absorb the time magic from it and skip all the extra steps?

I had to stop the thought train on that one.

I'd learned that nothing worthwhile came from cutting corners, no matter how impatient I was I was determined to do it right.

I pulled my T-shirt over my head and ran my fingers through my hair quickly before walking up to the chest.

"Be careful now, love." Silas said endearingly.

It made me smile as I nodded.

My heart thudded loudly in my chest as I crept toward the chest, Silas' warning still fresh in my ears.

I nudged it with my foot, making sure that it wasn't a trap or that it wasn't going to explode on me before I lifted the lid and groaned.

"You're sure this is where the sand clock is?" I sighed.

"Yes." Silas said surely. "My entire life I'd known that what was in that chest was the key to complete control of the element of time."

I reached down and picked up the chest's only content— a shining golden key that matched the glimmer of the chest.

I held it out for Silas to see, but the second my skin touched it there was a flash of golden light and a door appeared in front of the chest, in the middle of the room, not even connected to a wall.

Silas and I exchanged confused looks.

"Maybe it's an added security measure?" Silas shrugged but his tone didn't sound like he was too convinced either.

I should have known that it wasn't going to be that easy. The universe was a fickle thing and I should have expected no less than a fucking maze of obstacles to break the time curse.

The door held a single, shimmering keyhole and the key practically vibrated in my hand.

So I took a deep breath and brought it to the door. The key slid into the hole perfectly and I held my breath, turning the key as slowly as possible until I heard the locks in the door shifting. The key turned all the way and I twisted the nob.

Whatever was behind the door was the key to fixing the shit show that was the time curse, but it was also the key to fixing the shit show of my life. It was the one thing I needed to be able to go back and rewrite my story the way it was supposed to be written. The key to finally finding peace and saving the world as we knew it.

I slowly pulled the door open and my heart sunk.

"What the hell?" I couldn't believe what I was seeing.

"What? What is it?" Silas peaked around the door and his face contorted with confusion too. "This can't be right." He stuttered.

In the closet, leaned up against the wall was Asher.

At least, it looked like Asher, minus the scar through his eye.

He was sleeping or enchanted, I couldn't tell which.

All I knew was that my mind was severely fucked.

"Is this a joke?" I asked.

The second the words fell from my lips Asher's eyes popped

open, filled with a glowing blue light.

There was a surge of magic that exploded from him and washed over everything in all directions.

I had to plant my feet firmly to keep from getting blown back.

Around us the candle lights started to flicker again, and I could hear birds chirping from outside.

Voices drifted from somewhere far off down the hall, ones that I'd never heard before.

"He broke the bloody curse!" Silas said in surprise.

Asher awoke from his magical coma and stumbled out from the closet.

If this is Asher, who the hell was on the TV screen burning everything to the ground?

"Who are you and where the hell am I?" Asher's hair erupted into wild flames.

Here we go again.

Printed in Great Britain
by Amazon